ANATOLI SCHOLZ

If Cats Could Talk... Would They Cry?

A NOVELLA

First edition

Cover & illustrations by Felix Diaz de Escauriaza
Edited by James Magniac

www.anatolischolz.com

To all cats who miscalculated their jump, fell down and then played it off as if nothing happened.

If Cats Could Talk... Would They Cry?

Life has but one true charm: the charm of the game. But what if we're indifferent to whether we win or lose?

Charles Baudelaire

On the morning of the 17th, after a particularly sleepful night, Julie Galles woke up to find herself transformed into a cat. Still half asleep, she watched a set of ginger and white paws stretch out on the beige duvet cover and felt every inch of her body yearning for a good scratch. She yawned and shook her head, a set of gray whiskers flickering in the corners of her eyes. Overcome by a sudden tedious thought, she took a gander around the room, followed by a relieved exhale on the note that nothing else had changed. Her little studio apartment was the same she had left it the night before.

The sun was up. It was glistening through the dirty glass

of Julie's apartment window and formed bright lines on her bed. The smell of red wine from the almost finished glass on her bedside table was mixing with the crisp morning air sliding through the cracks in the old wood frames. Turning herself to align with a sunny spot, the warmth bewitching her mind to an instinctive shuteye, Julie fell back asleep. Whether human or cat, there was no conceivable rush to get up.

Not that anyone could begin to judge her for taking a moment to relax in her studio on the sixth floor of the crooked apartment building number 54 on *Rue des Martyrs*. Tiny, yet well-furnished, the studio had a touch of what some would call a bohemian charm. Decidedly far removed from the type of bohemians that actually had money, Julie lived a humble life; it marked itself by thrifty way of presentation, accentuated in a modern admiration for woven things and antique stuff. It had been Julie's luck that her landlady, Mme Dufront, had left the studio furnished with an assortment of cabinets, a decorated bed frame, and one perfectly pink chaise longue that may as well have belonged in the courts of Versailles. All of that was nestled inside the fittingly dolled up green and turquoise facade of block 54. Myth would have it been the domicile of an illustrious brothel that ran the first two floors in the seventies. The question of whether its proprietor was the very same Mme Dufront was never actually answered.

A sharp noise tore Julie from her first feline slumber. A ringing and a humming bore itself into her ear. It came from underneath the pillow. Julie jumped, extending her new claws into the softness and ripping into the fabric. The source sounded small but didn't scare from Julie's fierce attack, continuing to ring and tune. Julie put her face down and slid her paw under the pillow to try and brush the culprit out from there. Once she managed, she sat back up and watched her bright metallic phone lie in front of her, shaking her head at each vibration it made. A few seconds passed with Julie staring at its blinking light until she felt it right to push it over the edge of her bed.

Be gone, she thought, watching it glide off. *Annoying thing.*

But the phone landed with a quiet "Hello?" as Julie's dismissive tap had accepted the call. She followed the ejected object, stretching her legs before jumping off the bed and surprising herself with a perfect landing on the carpet.

"Hello, Julie? Are you there?" said the voice on the phone. Julie recognized Mathilde, her boss from the *Galeries Lafayette*. She didn't sound as if she had the time to relax in the sun that morning.

"Julie, I can't hear you. Call me back right away! It's urgent! The Chinese are here! Where are you? Call me back!"

Toot-toot.

Julie kept looking at the phone until its light dimmed off. She yawned, closing her eyes slowly to look back up at her bed and then meowed. Of all of the things that she had experienced so far that morning, this was the one that startled her. She was struck by a million tiny realizations of what had just happened, wondering if she really did make that noise. She meowed a second time.

Julie did not want to panic, as it would have been unlike her. She was an expert in emotional compartmentalization. In other words, Julie had always experienced life's precious instances in small, digestible portions. If there had been any time or reason to panic, she would do so, but never unexpectedly or against her will.

Remaining seated on the carpet by her bedside for a quick minute, breathing calmly, and looking at nothing, Julie had all of her thoughts under control. Following a moment of clarity, when all of her first responses began to ebb away, she decided to walk over to the oval mirror by her cabinet and get a full look at what was going on. She approached the upwards-facing mirror, where she would normally be standing, tapped the bottom tip, and thus turned it at herself.

In the reflection, where for twenty-five years she had been met by the familiar freckles of her youthful face, the face of a ginger cat was now looking back at her. Her curly mane of red hair was replaced with lush and shiny ginger fur, dotted by white patches on her forehead and the ends of her paws. Behind her seated figure, a fuzzy tail waved back and forth at her as if luring a welcome into this new reality. She was a cute cat, she had to admit. Long whiskers, a slender figure, and an adorable little head, centered by a pink button nose. The reflection's green eyes she recognized as her own. Even though their vertical pupils weren't what she was used to, there was a familiarity in their warm hue that gave Julie comfort. Along with all of her past memory and the ability to perceive it as a reassuring detail.

The initial fright continued to wear off the longer she looked at her new reflection. Julie wondered if this had all been a dream, her human form swimming through the delta waves of her own imagination. Nonsense, she thought, a cat didn't think like a human, could it? It had to be a dream. If only the hairs hadn't stood up on her back at that exact moment. She felt her paws keeping the ground below, her hind legs standing up, the end of her tail brushing through the air, and the smells, the millions of new smells. If it were a dream, it was a mighty realistic one. She had to assume that it wasn't, for better or for worse, turning away from the mirror to get another view of her studio. From this point of view, the wooden frames and wall-length closets looked much taller and carried a different energy than usual. There was an air of adventure around objects Julie had barely noticed before. The shapes and smells of her landlady's old furniture were teasing her. In excitement, Julie licked her nose. Lavender, that sweet-purple scent of blooming lavender descended from the candle on her bedside table to fill her nostrils. And then a wave of old and new pages coming from her bookshelf; three yoga books, a yellow-leafed copy of Alexandre Dumas' *Monte Cristo,* and an illustrated collection of Haruki Murakami's short stories, gifted to her by her ex. The laundry basket she had thought to bring to the laundromat before opening her Bordeaux last night, a pair of socks by the entrance, and something delicious hanging in the air. It all collided in a carousel of smells firing neurons around her head. The room was more alive than she had ever felt it. She licked her nose once more and shook her head to prepare to take it in once more.

The lilies in her kitchen, a gift from her mother, smelled as if Julie was dipping her nose into the petals. The food that she had smelled came from down the hallway of her floor, chicken soup or soufflé, she could taste its thickness interrupted by a sudden clonking. Julie listened to the sound of footsteps rushing through the courtyard, six flights down. She could even hear the drops of water from her runny faucet. It was a concert!

Julie jumped onto the chair and back to her sun-drenched bed. She laid down on her back and stared onto the ceiling. The white background calmed her senses. It was surprisingly easy to control, she found. Much easier than when she was human.

Any remaining part of her anxiety went away with this realization. Julie was proud of her resolute reaction. Although she hadn't asked for an entirely new set of pupils, a change in perspective was something she had been longing for. Maybe this was her great chance to explore the things she hadn't been able to for long. Either way, waking up as a cat was certainly better than waking up as some revolting insect. The warming rays of the sun continued to soothe her fur.

Just another morning.

Julie stretched her legs to reach for another sunny spot on her bed, making a note of a little rumble in her tummy - a predicament that would have to wait. She dozed off.

A loud knock on the studio door woke Julie from her second nap. She perked up her head and stared at the entrance behind her.

"Julie? Are you in there?" Spoke a female voice. Julie recognized Margot, her friend that also worked at the *Galeries* with her. Three more fast-paced knocks.

Julie looked down at herself and saw her ginger coat; still a cat. This was setting their friendship up for an interesting premier. She wasn't sure how Margot would react to her new form and hesitated to move. Margot wasn't always easy to deal with for Julie, finding her friend's dramatic reaction to the banalest mishaps already too overblown. Margot once kept the story of an unfilled coffee pot at work alive for about a week. Julie shuddered at the thought of what she would say if she found her friend all furry.

"Julie, are you there?"

The question repeated itself from the hallway, beginning to sound desperate. "Julie, it's me, Margot. People are worried. What's going on?"

Alright, alright, just give me a second.

Using her tail for inertia, Julie jumped back on the floor. An exquisite landing, once again. She approached the door and jumped onto the door handle in an elegant effort, allowing the door to slide out of its lock with a loud squeak.

The door opened, and Margot burst into the room, glancing down at Julie with negligible surprise and stepping around the studio with much else but a few Ah's and Oh's. She walked to the bed, then the kitchen, and back into the bedroom. Margot was wearing black ballerinas from Mango, a lacy light-blue dress, and a lost expression on her face. Julie observed it all seated by the entrance and

11

admitted to herself becoming entertained from seeing her become increasingly confused.

Margot's dress twisted around in sync with her bouncy brown hair as she made her quick bursts around the studio. Her presence did bring with it a heavy smell of cigarette smoke, which Julie felt right away but ignored until she had to sneeze.

"Julie? Where are you? And when did you get a cat?" Margot finally spoke into a seemingly empty room. She kneeled down to pet Julie, who began to lick her nose after the sneeze.

Julie wasn't sure how to help her friend or if she had any way to do so in the first place. She was sure that she didn't expect to enjoy the scratching and petting as much as she did. Julie closed her eyes and bathed in the scratches for as long as they lasted. She didn't want it to ever stop, reaching an unexpected level of calm.

"Margot, it's me," she muttered.

Half in ecstasy and half-expecting another meow, Julie's words came out of her in human tongue.

Margot pulled her hands back from the animal after hearing her friend's voice. She jumped to her feet with a look of panic and gave off one single high-pitched screech before starting to scream.

"What the hell? WHAT THE *HELL*? What is happening? Did you just speak?" Margot grasped her purse as if it contained anything helpful.

Julie stayed still, looking up at her friend, seated, and moving the end of her tail back and forth.

So I can speak, that's helpful.

Julie felt an immediate obligation to let her friend know

about the morning's revelations without much regard for its oddity.

"It's me, Margot. It's Julie, your friend", she got up and took a step toward a retreating Margot. "Please try not to panic, OK? It's all right. I'm just a cat, not a snake."

Margot looked struck, her face fading from an opaque blush-orange to a tone of translucent blue. Still holding her purse in a deadly grip, she pushed her back firmly against the wall behind her, visibly twitching between instinct and rationale. Her hands were shaking, and her eyes stopped blinking. From one moment to next, she gasped for air once more, mouthed a wordless prayer, and slumped down to the floor knocked out.

Well, that's just great. What a diva.

Julie was a little relieved by the return of silence but felt bad for her friend, trotting over to Margot's collapsed body. She had fallen in a most uncomfortable position. Only one of her knees had decided to fold, and both of her arms had somehow swung to her right side. It was an unflattering sight, unmarred by the beauty of her outfit.

"Why did you even come here?" Julie said out loud and began licking her friend's face. "This is what happens when you stick your nose into other people's business," Julie grumbled while her tongue tasted every layer of her friend's make-up. Margot crinkled her nose but otherwise went on with her involuntary sleep.

The revelation that she could talk moved into focus. Even though she had long calmed about the transformation, her growing hunger had started to worry Julie. She kept staring at her friend's resting face and saw the corner of her mouth curl to one side as if to tease her about it. A few more licks later and all they produced were more smiles. The taste of strange chemicals combined with the smell of chicken still lingering in the air and Julie hadn't the slightest idea what to do about it. Having the ability to speak and Margot show up at her doorstop was certainly going to help, but both of them needed to be awake. Simply asking her friend to give her something seemed more civilized than whatever uncivilized cats did. Scavenge, perhaps? She needed to wait until her friend came back to herself.

Despite her comments, Julie knew that Margot had been her closest friend for the last few years. The two had met five years ago working at the luxury perfume department of the *Galeries*. Aware of how dissimilar they were from the start, Julie often wondered if they would have stayed friends if it weren't for the circumstance of spending most of the week in the same building. Being a similar age and having the same affinity to social drinking and sexuality helped. It made Julie rather perceptive of the general notion of the word *friend*.

In return, Margot had also never shied away from mentioning her distrust toward some of Julie's heartless antics. She was more polite about it. But it enough for Julie not to feel bad about depending on her friend's provincial simplicity. Given that, it was unsurprising to find out how different their upbringings were. Margot had grown up with her family in Nevers, a village in the dead center of the Bourgogne, between hills of vines and landscapes filled with grasshoppers and lazy cows, by her own account. She would allude to it all in apology to her mother's frequent and frequently untimely phone calls, saying she simply didn't understand the schedules of city life. Julie laughed along, but mostly envied Margot for the fact that her mother only ever intruded on her daughter's life over the phone, unlike Julie's own mother, who always did her best to appear for her intrusions personally.

Margot had told Julie a few stories from her childhood that Julie found to mark all her relevant traits of her countryside naiveté. The rest Julie filled in with her own imagination. Young Margot and her sisters running down the village's old dirt road on a Saturday morning to get the breakfast bread for their father, who waited patiently on the veranda after an honest week's work. Rough hands and voiced by a heavy Portuguese accent, he had met his wife during the month he spent at the lumber processing plant in Limoges where she was from. Their affection had always been unattainably passionate and had resulted in at least one of their daughters' unrealistic expectations for her own love life.

Margot never asked too many questions about why things were the way they were. Just like that image of her childhood breakfast, Julie saw Margot live her life as told, excelling at chasing grasshoppers and getting bread. Anything that was in line with her idea of an adorable life. Julie had often watched her disappear back into that world in the middle of a workday. In between shifts or when the busy aisles of the shop would die down a little, Margot would hold still and smile into nothing. That's when Julie knew her friend was back there, probably running around a rolling hill of flowers and thinking of how wonderful it all was.

With other people, Margot's innocent character showed best during the usual lunchtime gossip. Julie remembered last spring when Margot undertook the unsolicited step to start a gossip completely by herself, a brave yet ultimately doomed undertaking. She told Julie and Yousri, their gay colleague from men's outerwear, that Emmanuel from discounted jewelry was paying his private weekend lunches using the company's credit card. While most would have agreed with this to have been somewhat dishonest, it did fall into that somewhat general category of "*et donc?*", French for "is this worth wasting my precious afternoon air?". But Margot insisted in how scandalous it was. She went on about honor and duty and how Emmanuel was morally flawed to haven taken advantage of their employer's trust like that.

As her friend kept on with the story, Julie wondered why Margot hadn't spiced it up to at least include buying a hooker or, better yet, burying one. It was unfathomable to her how Margot had remained so innocent even after years of city life. She had close to no scope on how to measure real darkness in character. Incidentally, it was later discovered that Emmanuel did enjoy the company of escorts in the staff changing rooms and was subsequently bumped up to chief buyer of the handbag section around Christmas.

What drew Julie to Margot still was their mutual oddness. Julie knew that Margot had overlooked as of Julie's shortcomings as she did with Margot. Beyond the worksite assistance, it made her aware of why they had to be friends. Julie would have preferred to see their friendship as more profound, maybe even someone she loved. Instead, at most times, it was simply comforting to have someone around who couldn't exploit her.

Julie had moved to the foot of her bed and had been

looking at Margot's collapsed figure to see if she moved. At least she had an amusing friend in her, Julie resolved. Margot's mouth curled up once more.

Julie looked away and eyed the top of her antique bedside table that had one of Mme Dufront's white embroidered cloths hanging over one side. While it hadn't been much more than a dust catcher before, its location next to the window had never looked as inviting as it did now in the stronger daylight. Julie leapt up on the bed and then onto the cabinet, curling up on the doily and taking a final look at Margot's sorry figure before shutting her eyes once again.

J ulie's hunger made it difficult for her to stay asleep. She kept jerking at each of Margot's loud snores until an inconspicuous cirrus cloud passing over her neighbor's rooftop caught her attention. She licked her left paw, and then her arm. Unsure of why she was doing it, Julie lured herself into a kind of hypnotic state that made her forget about her empty belly. The cloud passed, her fur soothed, and her glance fell below the sky across the courtyard. The window across framed the image of her neighbor shaving in his bathroom, half-naked. The novelty of the spectacle made Julie understand how little she cared. Unaware of the observation, the neighbor stared into the familiar reflection of his bathroom mirror, moving a satisfied face from side to side and then rattling the razor in the filled sink. Water trickled over its edges and Julie understood that it wasn't for her to worry anymore. She no longer had to stress about the visibility of her own bedroom, her job, or how others thought of her. No more need to be nervous about the Chinese or guilty about the dozens of unanswered messages filling her dating apps. It was more than she could ever have wished for.

Living in Paris for a long time had the common side-effect of acting like a bitch in your everyday interactions. As much as Julie had hoped to evade this fate by avoiding everyday interactions altogether, there was no escape in the mayhem. She tried to be nice at times and had even spun the wheel of social relevance. She had kept up with societal waves of unironic enthusiasm toward designer moisturizer or Ashtanga yoga but never knew for what purpose. She always found herself pretending to feel their rush and, in that, very lonely. On top of that, the only council she had ever sought, Maman, had made her fully believe that there was something seriously wrong with her, so she stopped complaining. Luckily for her, Paris allowed this way of life to flourish as well: to be either shyly withdrawn or coldly cynical and not to stand out in the slightest. Everyone was so self-centered that Julie doubted anyone ever noticed anything around them. She imagined being able to walk into her downstairs *Café Brutte* as a cat, ordering a coffee, and no one would even bat an eye. In a city where one is polluted and pollutes others with the wildest ideas at a bewildering pace, there's no filter to tell what is worthwhile and what is a rotting sardine. Julie wanted to believe that she wasn't the only one to suffer through this tonal split, but had yet to see any proof. What she believed to see in others was a kind of happy involvement or willful ignorance, which, more than anything, she actually envied.

Julie lived at the foot of Montmartre, Paris' artist district of old, the epicenter of this restless experience. Here, cultural vagabonds tried to upstage one another at each corner leading to the topping basilica. Painters painting portraits of young tourist couples on the *Place du Tertre* while the Edith Piaf impersonator piped "*Milord*" twenty times in a day. Julie couldn't hide a smirk when she thought of the vanity of the artists in the prospect of money. There was a symphonic swing in the shackles of shekels on Montmartre, where everything hid behind the great coulisse of art, one day to emerge as butterflies on center stage, virtuous and brilliant. Until then, commerce talked. It had helped to push Julie into that lasting limbo, a frantic and anxious stupor, searching for answers in fruitless jobs and unfulfilling partnerships. Maybe that was what she realized when she saw her neighbor. The simple kindness of a window that she never found the time to look out of as a human. With each year, she had shed more and more of the inner child. That inner desire to do something different. Julie wished to have an urge to create anew or be swept away by the adventures of life. More often, she wished to simply care for something or someone without scaring herself. Just the idea seemed an illusion.

Julie's hunger returned to pull a full stop on her mental spiral. She jumped down from the cabinet with a loud meow and pranced over to Margot, climbing onto her forearms to see if that would wake her. Margot let off a loud snore but kept snoozing.

Feeeed me!

Julie entered the kitchen and looked around to see if her past self had been so kind to have left any food lying around. She looked up at the kitchen window. The sun was coming straight in, illuminating the tiled room into a gallery bright white. It must have been early afternoon and, therefore, high time for lunch. Julie's eyes scanned the kitchen for food once more, fixating on the fridge.

Her hunger triggered an animalistic concentration. She jumped onto the kitchen counter and sniffed around its corners until she bumped into a cling-wrapped Tupperware box by the sink. She remembered the left-over ham from yesterday's sandwich. Julie ripped into the loose wrap with her claws and played with the box until it flew off the counter. When it landed, the lid came off, and its contents spilled out. Julie jumped down and began to devour the sweet meat promptly, having turned into an uncivilized scavenger after all.

The satisfaction of stilling her hunger transcended the animal form on all levels and Julie felt happier on the spot. She sat there on the tile floor, her belly filling slowly, licking her whiskers and cheeks, and returning to her wandering thoughts. It seemed fair to think that things had changed now that she had become a cat. No one could expect her to care about how she looked, her past, or Montmartre any longer.

There had certainly been a cut in her life since the morning. Julie looked down at her ginger and white paws, the taste and smell of ham still lingering around. She asked herself if there was anything she did not like about the transformation, anything she missed from being a human. She tried to remember what it was like to be one in the first place.

A memory cleared Julie's mind like a sunrise brushing through the morning fog. Julie remembered her walk to primary school in *Saint-Ouen*, holding a familiar Tupperware in her hands, and the touch from her mother's kiss still cooling on her cheek. It was a moment she hadn't thought about in a long time.

Julie stood in the courtyard of her elementary school at the edge of the sandpit at the beginning of her second year. Maman had to come see her from the office because Julie had left her lunch in the car. She had just enough time to see her daughter when she turned and ran back because a bus stalled behind her car left on the curb. Julie's classmates came up to her and asked if that had been her mother. She remembered feeling annoyed by their inquiry, their baseless curiosity, but standing quietly by the sandpit, looking down at her lunch box.

Getting no reply, Julie's classmates lost interest in her and took no time to return to jumping between the penetrating plastic sculptures and wooden shapes of the playground. All but one of them. Eloise, the only other redhead in her class, came up again to ask Julie to join in the game, tugging at her hand to help her friend out of her stupor. Using all the arguments available to a child, she tried to move Julie with stricter demands, but nothing worked. Eloise didn't understand that Julie wanted to disappear, for the sandpit to open up and devour her without anyone noticing, for her to just be left alone.

Julie remembered seeing her life from the outside for the first time. Time stood still for seven-year-old Julie and played out in front of her like one of her cartoons. Her friends hopping around while the teachers looked on and how she stood there, a character in folds of her tempting friend, a shy explorer of a new world. She could not be moved to play, despite her outrageous curiosity. She sat down and watched as even Eloise gave up trying and her mind could cool down from this internal tear.

Julie felt the odd one out that day, and the day after, and for all the days that followed. Without knowing it then, this distance, this shyness was going to become Julie's defining feature. Over the course of her childhood, she rarely played with other children, easily able to account for each occasion on which she did. She avoided diving into social situations that others found interesting, comfortable in looking at the swing set from afar. She would have even gotten comfortable with the strange looks if it weren't for her mother. Once *Maman* had observed Julie's oddity, she never stopped trying to get Julie to join the others, to play with them, and pretend to like it even if she didn't. *For goodness' sake*. It wasn't any help that Julie's little sister Anya was running literal and figurative circles around her older sibling. Anya, who was only one year younger, was Julie's polar opposite. She would jump around and join every game in her reach, feeding into their mother's persistence with Julie. Julie felt Maman's piercing side glances even as she was mostly focused on Anya, who would drive her mother crazy with other things, her daring stunts, teasing, and even hitting other children. And still, Maman would call Anya more normal.

Julie's father didn't care as much about the playground's rules and expectations, or possibly anything. As a postal worker, his employment demanded him to be social, but Julie saw that he did not let that affect him. After work, he would often sit on the balcony for hours, observing passersby or reading, disconnected from the reality of their house. He would not mind being interrupted by the odd request but would return to his favorite chair once all household chores had been cleared. It was his favorite pastime, and Julie had no memory of him going out with friends or being around many people. Just like herself, he seemed to prefer being alone.

When he spent time with his daughters, he would often tell them stories about fantastical worlds he seemed to enjoy far more than the girls. Often meddled with his favorite Greek myths to the point where the characters blended completely, it was the most animated Julie would ever see him. He usually told them as bedtime stories, sitting between the beds of the two sisters and relaying the myth of how Apollo guided the postcard of his brother Silvain in

Massalia. He would get up with his booming voice and act out how the postcard arrived at the feet of the mighty Myrmidon warrior François in time to save both princesses of Troy.

It was no surprise that Julie grew closer to him than her mother. Whenever Maman complained about her daughter's shyness, he would call Julie over to sit on his lap and whispering into her ear: *You're a philosopher in the making.* Maman would scoff at them, but his words stuck with Julie. She adored that he saw her in this way. She did not think about it much at the time but remembered perfectly how his face pulled tighter as he spoke these words, full of conviction and nodding in encouragement.

Julie's father was a tall man with a dark, Mediterranean expression. Most of his speech was accompanied by a hearty but tired smile. Every time Julie thought of him later on, she understood more of his face: profound, but utterly misunderstood in this world. On their last family vacation together to the Normandy, Julie's family was visiting her maternal grandparents, he had barely made the train. He countered Maman's stinging comments by reminding her that he came from the south of France and how much it meant for him to visit those cider drinkers in the north. His daughters ought to know what a kind heart he is to do so, he said. Seeing his wife's reaction, he added that he loved the ocean no matter where it was.

At the beach, the family walked down to the break at low tide. Maman always talked. She commented on the other beach-goers and her advancing flower categorization, neither of which interested Julie. She wanted to listen to her father, who would speak less but made it count. She felt that he knew so much more to say of what she wanted to hear.

On that day, in a moment when her mother walked ahead with Anya, her father turned to Julie and pointed at the ocean. She was young, and even though she didn't know what was going to happen, Julie felt a new ease in his voice. Still, she was left no way to deal with it when it all happened. She couldn't remember any family talk, no school counselor, or comforting grandparent from the countless hours she spent with them afterwards. The only thing she remembered was the five seconds it took him to speak the words when he pointed to the ocean that day:

"Look at the waves, Julie. They are like men playing in the curls of the gods."

Julie was thirteen years old when her father left the family. Following a few escalated arguments with Maman, he had taken a position to run a regional office on Reunion and never returned. Just as the memory of her moment at the sandpit was clear, all she remembered from that time was the feeling of uncertainty creeping into every corner of her life. As her dearest person in her life disappeared, she grasped the importance of the choices that lay in front of her. At that time, although it shook her deeply, she felt she knew why he had left, but kept it to herself.

Maman was left no choice but to start accepting Julie to hold the family together. At the same time, Julie started to accept the way of living life in boxes, modeling herself after him. She had observed him long enough to know what she had to do to be a part of this world.

Those were surely human moments. Possibly her last that were profoundly human before losing her innocence to everything that engulfed her. Julie put on a face for all of them every day since, covering her lingering curiosity and shy disobedience. It was a face that hid all sentimentality to seem stronger. It felt as if she had committed to a lifelong conspiracy against herself. It was easier than admitting to everything she saw. After all, she had been flying under the radar for a while, and everything had been going fine, really.

Julie had done her best to live a prescribed life. She joined the playground games, eventually. She did what was asked of her, coerced into normality. As a result, she couldn't remember the last time she could tell weeks apart, let alone days. Her runs around the sun mixed into an alphabet soup of moments of things that possibly happened but had no lasting importance. She probably could have done something to stop it, but never did. In time, Mondays rolled into Wednesdays and onto the last day of the month until it was already Christmas. At the very least, there was no pestering visibility in that type of life. No staying up late hoping for that long-distance phone call. It was a comforting lull. She had not even considered this feeling to ever stop or change, or for a spark to reignite her curiosity. Until this morning.

Julie felt that her catamorphosis played into her hands. This was her opportunity to break a vicious cycle and return to her internal affairs without sticking out for everyone to see. A smirk sketched itself across her furry face. It took her turning into a cat to think about being more human.

A cat didn't really care what day of the week it was. Julie had understood that almost immediately. All that mattered to her now was a good scratch, some food, and a healthy dose of quiet. Her whiskers bent up to another smirk. Yet, something had changed, and Julie was starting to grasp what it was. Her life, her endless game of waiting for something to pass, had reached a feline interlude. There was something almost frightening about it. Her formal liberty intimidated her. If this was what she had waited for, she didn't recognize it. That wishful break had always lived in a delicate balance between a certain future and ignorance about its form. She never expected it to actually appear, and now that it did, she wasn't sure what to do about it.

Looking around, Julie's eyes fell on the closed door of her apartment. She immediately thought of her father's story about Artemis, the protector of wild beasts. Her bow would tear through the ropes of the bound, and her horn called upon hordes of boars to stampede through the battlefield. What kind of a cat would Julie be if she remained locked inside?

She jumped down from the counter and walked over to Margot, tapping her friend's leg. A trusty assistant would go a long way in her plans.

"Hey! Hey!" Julie yelled, her voice sounding higher than normal. Margot didn't move. "Margot!" She cried as loud as she could, with no reaction. Julie hesitated to scratch Margot's arm or even nose but did not want to push this morning's series of surprises.

There was a knock on the door. A short silence, and another. Julie jumped at the banging and was at once surprised that she hadn't heard any footsteps approach. Meanwhile, Margot awoke from the second knock. The previously motionless occupant blinked her eyes and ruffled herself up with a grunting noise. Margot stretched from a slouched position. She did not seem to remember what had happened or where she was but walked straight to the door by instinct. She took a short moment to fix her hair and rub her temples, then reached for the handle to see who was there.

"Julie?"

A high-pitched voice sounded from behind the door before Margot could even open it.

"I heard someone scream a minute ago. Is everything all right in there?" She spoke in English.

Julie sat down by her bed, partially covered by her duvet, and watched Margot open the door to the little blonde British exchange student who lived next door. The poor girl still had last night's makeup smudged across her cheeks. Julie had met her on the odd occasion in the stairwell or the Lendemain bakery downstairs. She was always actively avid about something, a truly un-Parisian quality.

"Everything is quite all right. I just stubbed my toe," Margot responded briskly, adding a "thanks" and closing the door as the girl's gaze started to scan the inside of the flat.

"Oh…all right then. I just wanted to check. Is Julie with you? Can I help with anything? Do you need any bandages?" The girl insisted as the door closed on her.

"No, thanks. Bye."

"Bye!"

Julie thought she heard Margot mumble something in front of the closed door where she remained. Both of them listened to the once-energized steps of the neighbor return to their nest down the hallway.

Margot turned back toward the room and looked around. Her forehead wrinkled as she took a confused gander at the studio. Julie assumed that she must have started to remember what had happened. Indeed, Margot's eyes slowly changed from a thoughtful look to being widened with alarm. Julie waited a few more seconds before coming out from under the duvet and prancing over to the kitchen without looking at Margot.

"Have you calmed down, now?" Julie asked in motion.

She tried to sound as nonchalant as possible to avoid any further shocks. "Was that the English girl from down the hall?"

"Julie?" Margot followed the cat into the kitchen. "Yes … your neighbor. She heard a scream … wait. What happened? Did I pass out? Am I …" Margot stopped talking. She took two steps to enter the kitchen.

Margot looked around, curling her eyebrows. She looked at the ginger cat on the floor in front of the sink. In her turn, Julie looked at her bewildered friend, walking over to her and curling her tail around her leg. Unwillingly, she started to purr, feeling a little embarrassed about it.

"Julie?" Margot asked, her eyes widening again.

"I hate to admit it, but I was getting bored with you laying around," said Julie. She looked up at Margot, stopped moving her tail, and jumped onto the kitchen counter.

Margot's eyes were peeling at Julie, looking as if they would fall out at any moment. She did not speak but held herself together this time.

Julie felt a satisfaction in seeing Margot's face. Its expressive and surrendered stare gave her situation a more glorified feeling than when it simply passed out. Once again, she succeeded in remaining a threat to her friend's reality. Margot was a straight thinker, as much as she was bungling, so that any variation from her usual life required some time to adjust. Margot felt more at ease being a human than a cat, and that was saying a lot. Her inspiration did not lie in the mysterious. She functioned on clear as day instructions and absolutely no last-minute changes.

"It's alright, Margot. I was, too, surprised …" Julie said to break the silence, even though it wasn't fully true. She waited to transition Margot out of her fear and continued to talk slowly. Margot took a step toward Julie, remaining an arm's length away from her.

"Are you feeling better?" Julie asked.

"J... J...Julie?" Margot stuttered. The next few words came out of Margot in the most silent timbre Julie had ever heard her friend speak. "Why...why are you a cat, Julie?"

"Why am I a cat?" Julie replied and had to giggle. It sounded like a skipping record. "I have no idea, Margot. I just woke up like this. But please, I would appreciate you not making a big fuss about it. I've been waiting patiently for you to open the fridge for me before I can go out. Do you mind?"

Margot laughed nervously. Julie did not think her answer was that funny and was genuinely craving something to drink. She was not going to be patient with Margot forever.

"Not a big fuss? My best friend is a cat! Am I dreaming?" Margot pinched herself.

Julie jumped at Margot and tapped her on her revealed forearm, scratching her skin open, but mostly to tease her friend out of her stupor.

"Ow!" Margot screamed, grasping her arm with the other palm.

Julie walked back to the edge of the counter and sat on her hind legs as if nothing happened.

"You're not dreaming, Margot."

Margot slumped into one of the kitchen chairs, holding her arm in pain. She looked both shocked and embarrassed. It was just a matter of time before everything would sink in and Margot would have to be ready to admit to what the real problem was.

"Could you help me with the milk, please?" Julie continued, ignoring the pain written on her friend's face.

Margot got up, still looking at Julie, but followed her instructions without asking any more questions.

"She wants milk…" Margot's voice sounded as if she was suppressing tears.

The refrigerator door finally opened. Again, without any solicitation, Julie meowed. She did not move or say anything but felt her friend freeze for a moment.

Margot proceeded to pour the milk into one of the bowls from the cabinet and put them on the kitchen table. She looked at it for a second, then down at Julie, and then back to the bowl on the table until she put the bowl on the ground next to Julie and sat back down by the kitchen table.

Julie didn't say anything, bowed over the bowl, and started slurping up the milk. It tasted delicious. She could feel the end of her ears twitching.

A few moments passed with the two friends occupying the kitchen in silence, only interrupted by the sound of milk dropping off of Julie's whiskers. Finally, Julie lifted her head from the bowl.

"Is it something you ate?" Margot asked, immediately as she made eye contact. "How could you just wake up as a cat? It's not something that just happens to people."

"And yet here we are," Julie answered, looking up at her friend. "Anyway, what kind of food do you think turns people into cats, Margot?"

Margot nodded along, with an absentminded look on her face, clearly not listening. Maybe it meant that she was starting to concede to the fact that her friend was indeed alright. Margot may have been stubborn, but not too strong-willed. Julie knew that Margot would rather continue to be worried about her than feel responsible for the situation.

"So, what do we do? Do we call the doctor?" Margot asked. She sat on the chair, leaning on her knees, looking straight at Julie, who had remained by her bowl.

"Actually, Margot, I was thinking I would like to get out of the city!" Julie said. "I've had enough of Paris. It's been too long since I left, and it's no place for someone like me."

"Leave Paris?" Margot countered. "To go where?"

"Out."

"As a…?"

"As a cat, yes. Especially as a cat. I won't miss the looks." Julie jumped onto the windowsill, where the sun was shining down brightly. A few birds were chirping outside.

"What looks? But people will look even more! You're a cat! A talking cat?!"

"I'm not planning to introduce myself to anyone, Margot. I just want to get out of here. Slip out, to be honest."

Margot's face took a tormented expression. She wanted to help but must have sensed that it was pointless to worry for someone who was showing no sign of trouble. Julie was waiting on Margot to concede to her call to action.

The bird calls became louder. Julie rolled onto her feet and peered through the half-opened window. Seagulls were rotating around her neighbor's rooftops, and a whiff of fresh air came through. Julie wished the birds would have been accompanied by an ocean breeze. Margot made a sudden move in her chair.

"Let me call Clément!" She pointed her finger up.

Julie reacted by stretching on the sill and moving her

head to the side and roll her eyes at her friend. "Why the fuck would you do that?"

"He might know what to do."

"I already told you what to do. Please leave your boyfriend out of this."

Margot looked at Julie, who held her head upright while lying on the windowsill. Julie tried to put on as determined a face on her as a cat's could be.

"Fine," said Margot, clenching her teeth. "Either way, I think he's cheating on me."

"Margot, we went over this a million times. He is. I told you he is." Julie meowed again, this time happy about the timing.

"Yes, but I told you, I think Anya made it up. I don't believe her. I believe him…I want to believe him…"

"Margot, you need to find yourself someone who actually cares for you." Julie didn't let her friend finish. "Someone has to tell you the truth. He's a bastard … and you know it. Can we go now?"

Margot remained silent. She perched herself back on the chair, looking to the side, and crossing her arms.

Julie had no interest in this conversation and was starting to see if there was any way for her to get on without her friend. She could have tried the door again or maybe sneak out the window but couldn't imagine the trouble she would run into later. The food hunt inside her own apartment had already been hard enough. No, she needed Margot to help her get out, even if it meant to consult her about her relationship. If she wanted to talk to Clément, she at least had to do it Julie's way.

"You know what you need?" Julie asked.

"What?" Margot sounded grumpy.

"You need that Latin lover I have been telling you about."

"Oh god, Julie! I don't want to hear this now! You're disgusting! I know what I want and what I don't want when I see what I don't want. And I don't want that." Margot replied with sass, but Julie saw her grin. Both friends looked at each other, and Margot let out a laugh.

"You know I am right," Julie added, licking her paws. She used the short pause in her friend's laughter to ask the important question. "Will you take me out of Paris now?"

"You won't let go no matter what I say, won't you?"

"I need to leave."

"I can't take you anywhere. I have to be at work later."

"Boring, Margot! Your friend is a cat, you can't take a day off?"

Margot looked at Julie and smiled. Suddenly, Julie had a new idea, something even better than leaving Paris, a clear vision of billowing trees and emerald meadows.

"Take me to Monceau!" Julie exclaimed. "It's a 30-minute ride. You can't say no to that."

"What?"

"You can take me to Monceau, can't you? At least I'll get out of here and into nature."

Julie watched Margot wriggle in her chair as she understood that she had little to oppose the offer. Julie's idea was bulletproof. Monceau was only a few metro stops away and decidedly within Margot's comfort zone.

"What exactly do you want me to do?" Margot asked.

"Just come with me, in case I need help. It's my first day in a cat's body. I know it doesn't seem like, but it's all quite new to me."

Margot got up and tapped her fingers on her thighs, looking for something.

"I need a smoke…" she mumbled to herself, loud enough for Julie to hear.

"Oh please, Margot, if you need to smoke, go outside."

"Do you mind?"

"Just be quick."

"I just need a moment to recollect myself."

"Yes, yes, don't worry."

Julie could see that Margot's started to shake. She felt bad for her but couldn't do anything. It seemed a curse of the newly transformed to deal with their unprepared friends. In her silence, Margot seemed to have agreed to her proposal, and Julie would have done anything for it to remain that way.

"I'll be right back," Margot said.

"Can't wait," Julie replied.

Margot gave her one last look at the door before she took out a cigarette and put it in her mouth with a quiet "this is all right." Julie turned her head back to the seagulls in the window as the door fell shut.

Earlier in the week, everything had started as it always did. Julie had to dig through her weekend clothes that lay stacked on top of last week's weekday clothes to piece together an outfit for the workday. It never seemed to work out to wash and sort her clothes before the week started, resulting in an unchoreographed swan dive into the bustling life of the *Rue des Martyrs* outside her apartment building.

Up toward Montmartre, the fish vendors cleaned their storefront, all wearing matching aprons and red flannel shirts. Down the street, the businessmen marched at a quick and controlled pace, all sporting the exact same brand of round glasses. Julie gave a quick hello to Lucille, the homeless lady who made her home in front of the *Boulangerie Lendemain*. Lucille grunted her response and continued typing on her smartphone without looking up. Meanwhile, the line outside the bakery was already looping around the corner into the *Rue Manuel*, and each swing of the entrance door filled the street with the smell of fresh croissants.

It was all so real and engaging, as if done on purpose. Even though Julie felt like the only observer, she somehow felt inadequate. Possibly because of that. The light hangover from the two glasses of *Cheval Noir* the night before dragged her feet on this Monday. Each pair of heels clicked with the buzzing words of passersby to resonate for seconds inside her head. The smells of fresh fish and fresh pastry did not ease it either. As unpatriotic as she felt in admitting it, the hour was too early for croissants.

From the *Martyrs*, Julie walked down to *Rue Chateaudun* to face the least amount of noise, where her movie's soundtrack eased to an acoustic piano. The buildings here were tall and broad and without any shops. There wasn't much traffic, foot or otherwise, rare in this part of the city. The few honks that reached these streets had to travel two blocks down from the boulevard. The only clues one would find to explain this quiet quarter were the golden plaques reading *BANQUE* that shone onto the sidewalk from the side of the street.

It was a longer path, but Julie knew that by taking it she would end up directly at the *Galeries'* east entrance, where she was expected this morning. There was, however, a more frivolous reason she took this path. Julie wanted to see the tourist buses from afar. Five to ten buses lined the footpath along the *Rue de Mogador* at all times during the day. It was a sight the city wouldn't advertise in its guidebooks.

The wheeled monstrosities looked out of place with their shrill coloring contrasting against the red-gold Haussmannians. Squatting next to the picturesque buildings, each bus leaned into the footpath on the uneven road, like an uninvited guest peeking into your living room window. Julie found it very fitting, considering the hundreds of middle-aged passengers they brought along.

The Chinese were always the first in line before the galleries opened, as numerous as they were prudent in their waiting. Julie often imagined how they must have been shipped here straight from China, especially for the purpose of waiting in lines because none would ever give off any sign of annoyance or general discomfort. Julie's view of the buses gave her a first indication of what was awaiting her that day. It also meant that she had about ten minutes to observe the people she would be dealing with later. Ten minutes before leaping into a forced customer-employee relationship, she took her time to study the shoppers, guessing who would end up at her aisle and what they'd be asking.

That Monday, as Julie made her way past the crowd piled up in front of the galleries this Monday, she noted that it was smaller than usual. An earlier voice message from Mathilde informed her that three buses had been stopped at the Belgian border, but Julie did not bother to listen to the entire message to find out why. Ideally, it meant that her day was going to be less busy: a first soothing thought of that morning.

Julie's main task in the *Galeries* was to help clients around a multitude of luxury accessory stores. Having started in the perfume department, where she first met Margot, her list of seller's experiences now included also watches, purses, necklaces, earrings, jewelry of all kind, and even ornate belts. She had always dreamed of being paid for simply watching people, and while this job was not what she had dreamed of, watching people was one of its main parts. Just as with the bus-crowd outside the galleries, Julie always took one serene moment before approaching any customer in her little adult playground.

Julie's manager was a fifty-something-year-old lady named Mathilde Brassier. Mathilde was the definition of what Julie knew about fifty-something-year-old ladies in Paris. She was slim and elegant, forcing a forty-year-old exterior that looked like it required a lot of effort. Divorced two years ago, she was not always rational but always resolute in her decisions. Mathilde was of small stature, barely reaching over Julie's shoulder, and fittingly apt in controlling minor details in her work environment. There would often be a scene in one of the shops where Mathilde would lash out about a stain or asymmetrical placement of an Armani suit. Julie assumed that there must have been a lot of pressure on her from her superiors to behave that way and take it so seriously.

Their age difference made Mathilde take a mother-like approach to Julie, which neither of them ever truly fulfilled. Julie felt Mathilde trying to be a role model but just couldn't muster any considerable amount of admiration for her boss. Most significantly, Julie never thought to be doing her job out of some innate passion, contrary to what she kept hearing Mathilde say. Julie did find Mathilde remarkable as a fellow employee. The most remarkable in that was that Mathilde kept insisting on seeing structure in this type of work. In Julie's eyes, that was quite an accomplishment. Mathilde would go into lengths talking to Julie about the way in which the galleries are run must one day be reflected in her own life: scheduled and meticulously organized but with a human touch. As a result, Julie felt that most of her colleagues existed in a sort of organized chaos. Each of them bluffing to look as if they knew what they were doing long enough for people to believe them, including Mathilde. Julie never did point this out. She didn't want yet another mother-daughter relationship to grow sour.

On that Monday, the Nespresso shop on the ground floor had gotten a new delivery of coffee beans, and the entire ground floor smelled of ground coffee. It acted callously on top of Julie's light headache. On top of that, the *Galeries* would always keep its lobby lit in a heavenly bright glow with garlands and chandeliers sparkling from corner to corner, as the reflective surfaces of the floors and countertops and each piece of jewelry mirrored their light. Julie needed a few minutes to get her head right as she stepped in. She was not yet ready to listen to a client talk about anything. Especially if they needed to buy an equally expensive watch for their aunt's husband in Guangzhou because they had gotten them one a year before. Yet, somehow, it is always in these pristine moments of total presence that life calls on the quiet one from the audience to get up on stage.

Julie spotted a short, helpless looking man dressed in unflattering dark clothes standing in the middle of the Swarovski isle. He was clearly not there to draw any attention, and Julie wouldn't have even noticed him had he not been so isolated. Even then, it was somewhat miraculous not to have confused him for a disproportionate mannequin. Against her better judgment, but with a grade of curiosity, Julie walked up to the man.

"*Bonjour monsieur*, my name is Julie Galles. Can I help you with anything today?" Julie applied her trained approach.

The man turned his head with a lost look on his face but smiled and reached out to shake Julie's hand. She saw that his eyes were still wandering behind his dirty glasses as he focused his attention on her.

"Hello, I … I am … John," he answered with a light accent. "I am just visiting after the meetings …" He looked like a man woken from a deep sleep.

"Can I help you with anything?" Julie repeated. "Are you looking for anything in particular?"

"I don't know. I just wandered in. You know, it's my first time. I've been to Paris many times before. But I never made it to the Galleries. Strange isn't it?" he said, ignoring Julie's questions. He took off his glasses, rubbed them, and slid them back on his nose.

"Nothing strange, sir. You are not the only one," Julie answered, trying to brush past the odd response.

"Yes … I see. Here, I thought I might be unique." John smiled and took a long look at Julie. She returned his kind expression and thought about how just moments ago he had belonged to a larger convoy of clients she was trying to avoid.

"So, what brought you to us, finally?" Julie asked.

"I work with textiles. You know?" John answered, threading an invisible needle with his hands. "Usually we don't get any time off, but a meeting got canceled. It was nearby and thought that I should come here. My family friend was visiting last summer and said that …"

While he was talking, Julie's mind started to drift away. She wished it had been intentional, then maybe she would have known how to control it. Unfortunately, the trigger was something subconscious. Julie had to resort to what she always did when she no longer followed a conversation. She filled in the gaps with a fantastic vision of what the person could be saying. In the case of John, it wasn't anything creative. Her hangover was to blame. She could have thought of a story explaining the origin of John's misfitting clothes. A freak textile incident, involving wool gangsters and string car chases. He, John, may have been chosen to deliver an important message and had to appear out of place in this unfitting attire as a disguise, fooling a rival textile boss. Instead of all that, Julie imagined that John was talking to her about his mother. In all fairness, it could have been either, as Julie nodded along without listening.

"Yes?" John leaned back, widening his eyes.

"What?" Julie tried her best not to seem to be ripped out of her daydream.

"The rhythm. Do you agree about the rhythm?"

What the hell was he talking about?

"You're going to have to explain that to me one more time, John. I am sorry," Julie replied.

"I see…"

The small man looked Julie up and down, taking half a step closer. "I said there's a rhythm in this city. People feel more. Do you agree?"

"A rhythm?" Julie asked.

"Yes!" John yelled and leaned back, smiling from ear to ear.

Julie looked around to see if anyone had heard that. The galleries were loud, already since the morning, no one seemed to notice the pair at all. Julie looked back at John, who was standing with his arms spread apart as if he was going to invite her to dance. She had to let off a laugh.

"I am sorry, John. A rhythm in this city? But it's pure chaos!" she countered.

"Of course there's rhythm. Even here, in this store. Look around!" He guided his open hands to all the people in between the shiny objects of the *Galeries*.

"I don't know, John," Julie continued in a much quieter tone than him. "It seems that most people only care for themselves, especially here. You can't expect help from any-one, except if they want to sell you something. An 'all for none, none for all' sort of thing." Julie moved her eyes from side to side, shy at the level of honesty that came out of her.

"You have a strong ego," John countered. "That is true. We have that in China now, too. Everyone is looking for something for themselves. Even when they talk to each other, selfish and not willing to give anything up. And yet, here, you are romantics. Not just the romance of love, but the romance of friendship and mercy. We don't complain so much as you, especially to our elders, but you do it here! Everyone does it! It's a passion! A romance for life that binds everyone in a universal glue. It's not a harmony, but a passionate rhythm of egos!"

It was Julie's turn to look John up and down. She had not expected words like this from him, or anyone, on this simple Monday morning. As if to impress her more, he took off his glasses again and wiped them again with the side of his shirt. It gave them both a moment to regroup.

"Wait," Julie replied as John put his glasses back on. "That doesn't really make any sense. How can the egos be glued together? Wouldn't that contradict each other?"

"Yes. You are all disagreeing all the time…about everything!" John said and put on another smile.

"Exactly! We complain a lot and all the time! How is that a rhythm?" Julie asked, feeling confident about her point.

"Let me ask you something." John took a moment between sentences. "Do you get anything from these personal revolts that you're facing every day? Are they really for you? Or are they for everyone? When you complain to the baker about his bread being too stale, are you not looking out for everyone who buys bread on your street? When you tell your tailor that their work is uneven, would it not be a service to each one of his patrons that comes after you?"

His response made Julie smile.

"You are very idealistic." She smirked.

"Allow me to be idealistic, I am simply not ready to leave

44

this city of yours," he replied.

John's face took a melancholic expression. His glance rested on Julie but did not make her feel uncomfortable. She remained entranced by the conversation that had already made her forget about her morning of headaches and smells. John had managed to provide her with something she would never have expected. He had surprised her, right there, in between the Gucci and Dior products aisles.

In a moment when Julie took another look around to return to her reality, she noticed Mathilde out of the corner of her eye. Her boss was walking over toward her.

"So, John, what do you care to get for your neighbors back home?" Julie asked, nervously smiling at John, who remained impassive to her change of tone.

Mathilde had reached them before he could answer. "Hello, sir. *Salut*, Julie. How are you?"

"Very well. And you, Mathilde? This is John, who is looking to buy something for his neighbors back home. John, this is Mathilde, the head of the department."

John didn't flinch, continuing to look at Julie after a quick side-eye to Mathilde.

Mathilde looked at Julie and John, smiling. "I hope Julie is taking great care of you, Mr. John."

"Most certainly." He gave her a shy smile and another nod.

"Great, great." Mathilde's attention diverted to a larger group of shoppers by the busy *Café Pouchkine*. "Well, I'll leave you to it then, goodbye!" And she was already off to her next station.

Once Mathilde left, John spoke again. "See?" He grinned.

"What?" Julie was still following Mathilde's footsteps.

"Your colleague came by simply to tell you she's there for you."

"I think she came to check up on me. That's annoying."

"Are those exclusive?" he said and bent down to look for something in his bag.

Julie watched Mathilde turn back around from the group by the café and wave at her to approach. The rustling of John's bag made her curious. Julie hesitated between continuing their conversation and following Mathilde's invite. John kept looking in his bag, inside of which Julie could spy a few shiny objects before he took one of them out--a golden plastic cat. She had seen them all around Paris in the front window of stores as she passed, with one waving arm and Mandarin characters written on their sides. John held it out to her.

"It's a gift. It'll bring good fortune to you," he said.

After some more hesitation and considering the fact that it was likely not a very pricey gift, Julie took the cat and thanked John. She turned back to see if Mathilde was still calling her over. Julie made a gesture to John that it was her time to go and he gave her one last smile and nod of understanding.

"I have to leave now, too, Julie Galles. Time to leave Paris," he added, before slinging his bag back over his shoulder and walking toward the Mathurin's exit. Julie hadn't thought back on this encounter until the day of her transformation.

Julie tried to remember what she had done with John's plastic cat as she stared a hole into the door through which Margot had left minutes ago. She wasn't even sure if she ever brought it back from the *Galeries*. Not that it would be of much help, but it stumped Julie to feel how little she knew about cats. She had transformed into one without so much as an instruction manual or even a hint of what to do. It frightened her to think that she didn't know how to behave like a real cat. She had, of course, leapt out of bed and trotted around the studio, even meowed, but there was certainly more to be understood about this feline existence. Were she to meet one of her new kin, she might have been outright embarrassed.

Julie's grandmother had a cat at the country house in *Montebourg*. Julie didn't remember its name, but she did have some memory of the cat itself and how it spent its days. Its dark fur made it look like an evil spirit when it stepped between the rocks of her grandmother's vegetable patch. There was not much more to the memory, as it was an elusive cat. It would often disappear days on end, leaving the family to worry, only to reappear without any penance, not unlike a distant relative.

Julie panned away from the studio door and jumped back up on her bed, nesting herself in the crevice between the duvet and the pillow. She looked at the two dancing figurines on her bedside table. One black and one white figure curled into each other, resembling the long-necked silhouettes of the ancient world's section of the Louvre. Clay pots and drawings of cats displayed in the Egyptian section of museums, sitting next to the menacing faces of Iris and Anubis. In those halls, the cats seemed more mysterious than their gods. The gods, in their eternal fashion, looked resolute and distant, but the cats' presence was much more sentient. Modest pottery of a robbed world carefully tucked away behind the glass walls and guarded by an ever-apathetic guardsman. What honorable lives those guards lead unknowingly, working in the company of the eternals. Surely the pharaoh's priests had something different in mind when they meant for their demigod to be protected in the afterlife. Carefully lowering their bodies into a sarcophagus beneath a structure to survive millennia, only to have a languid guard shove their feet around them, occasionally warning a curious child not to touch the glass. Somehow the cats escaped this dreadful afterlife rebirth. Their dignity remained intact, glancing through the halls of museums around the world, still mystifying their visitors. The mummy might come to life and curse the humans, but who knew what mischief lay behind the pupils of an immortalized feline. Julie began to understand why the Egyptians revered the feline as something equally divine as their gods.

Out of the same window where she had seen her neighbor shaving an hour ago, a cloudless sky was claiming the city's afternoon. Julie thought of Steinlen's famous *Chat Noir* poster that hung on every student's wall in their first year of moving to Paris. A black cat towering over an artist's café with a yellow halo around its head. While Julie did live at the foot of Montmartre and holiness seemed a repeating trait, she wore a sparkling ginger coat with not a single black hair on her. There was also less ideal impressionism surrounding her life.

Julie never wanted to feel grand. If her shortened human

existence had made one thing clear, this had to be it. To be, but be merely common, had been her credo for a long time. She didn't see herself achieving greatness that was worth any real struggle at all. Julie had seen enough people suffer to get there, affecting no real changes, no more or less happy than before. She had hope that in this new form, she would continue to avoid this temptation.

When she was fourteen, Maman took the family to visit a monastery up a winding road outside the Cypriot city of Paphos. While Maman visited the church and nearby coffeehouse, Anya and Julie spent hours observing the hundreds of cats melting in the patchy shadows of the olive trees of the hillside. Julie was upset with herself that she didn't remember this earlier. In the monastery, nuns, likely not having enough humans to care for, looked after the cats. It made for a strange sight to see the while cowls of nuns dashing between the bushes, ushering together, and feeding hundreds of strays. The cats on their end made it look like it was the most natural thing in the world. That lightness, sizzling in the heat while having someone else work for you. At least there in Paphos, the cats were white and ginger-like Julie.

Whether as a human or a cat, her role was commanded by others, that much she could not escape. If they weren't taking care of her in some sun-flooded monastery on Cyprus, they expected her to join the playground games. But pharaohs, nuns, and Steinlen all believed to have control over the feline without ever truly knowing the cat. Being one now, Julie understood what that meant. She was infallible.

Julie licked her paw against the stroke of her fur.

Suddenly, her throat clenched up and the most discomforting feeling beset her. She began to gag and wheeze until she could no longer breathe, starting to cough and having her throat tighten around a lump. With one last cough that scratched all of her innards, a disgusting ball of hair fell out of her mouth.

Maybe not infallible.

As the hairball lay in front of her, Julie tried to think of that again. After all, she had been part of that same societal spiral. It was unfair of her to keep pharaohs to a standard she could not keep herself. Once or twice, she had tried to command others. Her few romantic relationships had all failed, not in the least due to some misunderstanding over who was in power.

Faint clouds made their gray shadows move across the floor and wall of the studio. Julie jumped down to sit in front of them and watch. Shapes flew past her slowly as if wound around a band. Her thoughts dissipated, and Julie concluded that if she had, in fact, become some sort of god, she'd be happy for her human part to disappear even further. Whatever this transformation had entailed, it was not massively tragic. Quite the opposite, so far, it had given her an opportunity to swim in long lost memories, which she hadn't done in years.

A noise came rushing down the hallway outside Julie's door. They rose from barely discernible the distinct clickclack of Margot's ballerinas, followed by the sound of keys and the door opening.

"Julie? I am back!" Margot put her bag to the side and looked down at Julie. "What are you looking at?" Margot asked with a cheerful voice, seeing Julie staring at the wall.

"The shadows. Are you ready to take me to Monceau?" Julie replied without turning around.

"One second, Julie. I had an idea."

"What?" Julie's intuition rang every alarm bell.

"You really have become a cat, haven't you?" Margot asked.

"What are you saying?"

"Well, I just want to make sure I am not dreaming." Margot put her arms up.

"Where are you going with this," Julie said.

"I wrote Clément…I didn't say anything, but I needed to talk to him," Margot said.

"Oh god, Margot. No!"

"I promise, not a word! I just needed to talk to someone. I didn't say anything, but I think he figured something was off. He knows me too well."

Julie arched her back, instinctively.

"I just needed to talk to him," Margot repeated.

"What did he say?" Julie asked.

"He said to call your mother."

"No! No, Margot! Please tell me you didn't! Please, Margot, please!" All of the hairs on Julie's back stood up.

Margot bit her tongue. "She'll be here in ten minutes."

Julie hissed.

A few weeks ago, Julie had gone to visit Ben on a whim, again. The following morning, she was lying in bed and playing with his cat Eli while he was making her breakfast. Although she cherished their relationship for its simplicity, it was nothing more than a physical affair. Ben belonged to a Dutch subsidiary of her company; they had met at last year's Christmas party in Antwerp. They had seen each other every few months since, on the occasion that one of them was passing by in the other's city.

Unlike her own little studio, Ben's place in Amsterdam was larger and more modern, built functionally. Julie heard him once describe it as minimalistic but wasn't sure whether he knew what it meant. The apartment had sporadic empty spaces, indicative of a lack of fantasy to fill them rather than intention.

He was loud and smart and walked with the confidence of a successful industrialist, although two years Julie's junior. He had always manifested his interest in her without shame and wasn't bad looking, so Julie didn't mind his association. There had, however, never been any depth to her feelings for him, this much she assumed he knew. It may have even been possible that Ben was in another relationship, so little did she know about him. Their interactions were business-like, concise, and usually ended by him running off to another matter.

On her way to see him this time, Julie had to sit next to a French family on the train, two energetic children and their exasperated parents. It may have been an opportunity for Julie to reflect on why she preferred emotionally distant affairs to something more meaningful, yet, in the brief moments of silence on the train, it was the apathy of the parents toward their wild children that stopped her from overthinking it. It wasn't as if Julie had been more lonely than usual, the timing had simply worked out. On a boring Wednesday night, she had been at home rewatching *La Dolce Vita* while swiping through one of her five dating apps when Ben wrote her. She was debating with herself about how screenwriters and directors believed in romantic love in such a way that possessed them to make these films, answering his message in that state of mind. She was caught in the middle of a melancholic review of her own life and a lover writing her. Julie was arguably defenseless.

"I could make it to Amsterdam next weekend," she wrote.

To which he simply replied, "Perfect. Come."

It was when she arrived at Amsterdam's *Centraal* that she began to have doubts about this trip. Taking the short walk from the station to the *Prinsengracht*, she felt that she made it too easy for him. Pausing in front of his door, she was already lifting her heals to turn and walk away, when he opened up. Ben welcomed her with his cocky smile, wearing basketball shorts and a white T-shirt. It was easy for her, too, she reasoned. With little resistance, Julie let herself be seduced to yet another dimly lit adventure in Ben's house by the canal.

Ben had named his cat Eli. Although Julie did not like the name for its religious connotation, she liked the animal. Eli became particularly cuddly with her when Ben would leave the room. The morning after her arrival, the cat jumped onto the bed while the two were still half-asleep. Eli's pale-white fur blended in perfectly with the bedsheets. Moving calmly, he snuck up on Julie so that when he touched her hand, it gave her a small fright. His pink-rimmed light blue eyes stared right at her as she turned around. Ben seemed not to have noticed him. He turned around and looked at Julie with one hand snug between his cheek and pillow.

"Hi there." He shuffled a little closer. "What a sight, first thing in the morning."

"Nicer than this little one?" Julie replied without looking at him, playing with Eli.

After a short silence, Julie looked over and saw that Ben must have wanted to cuddle and her quip cut him off. He had turned onto his back. She had noticed something different about him this time, something intangible that hung around since her arrival the night before. Now that the physical part was over, the confrontation was more potent.

Julie looked over at Ben, who was still making a point of not looking at her. She felt no need to insist on his attention. The game of string with Eli was intensifying. When she hid the string under the covers, Eli looked Julie in the eye, as if to tell her to stop teasing him. She was amazed at this skill. Having the ability to communicate purely through eye contact, every relationship based on what it could say through those light pupils. There was no need for verbal complications or clarifications. His eyes could rest on Julie for just a little longer to show his disdain for hiding the string, or maybe it was disinterest.

"You're not very sensitive for a girl sometimes, you know?" Ben spoke up. He turned onto his elbow.

Julie looked at him. "What do you mean?" she asked.

Ben didn't say anything, got up, put on his glasses, and walked over to the kitchenette. It was a few steps away behind a thin wall on the left side of the bed.

"Not what you are thinking," Ben continued, barely audible.

"Well, I am curious now, tell me. What do you mean?"

"Sensitive, elegant, whatever." Julie heard Ben from behind the thin wall.

"Right, so now I am also not elegant?" Julie sat up demonstratively and raised her voice.

"That's not what I mean."

"Then what do you mean?" she asked, knowing he had dug himself into a hole.

"I guess it's more of a state of mind." Ben peeked his head out from behind the wall. "You know, like a state of affairs. You don't seem to care about it. You know how to be sensitive when you need to be, and you are. But the moment it's not necessary, you switch it off as if it wasn't a part of you."

"Stop with your bullshitting." Julie went back to playing with the string on the added real estate.

"No, come on!" Ben continued, unfazed by Julie's absent tone, dimming his voice behind the wall again. "I'm serious. I don't know what to think sometimes. Whether you are here because you want to or it's just by chance. Like, if you wouldn't have heard from me then, I wouldn't have heard from you at all." Julie heard him put on the kettle. "You know what I mean?"

Julie smelled a freshly opened bag of peppermint tea. Ben didn't ask her if she wanted any. Maybe it was his way of telling her that she was not to feel in control. Eli, suddenly uninterested, jumped down from the bed and walked over behind the wall as well. Julie slipped out of her covers and followed the cat.

"Always talking," she said and hugged Ben from behind. He turned around and kissed her on the cheek. She had

57

already forgotten what he was saying, running her hands along his half-naked torso.

Making lasting connections with people had always been difficult for Julie. She never knew how someone could have the courage to look for a friend, or simply walk up to someone, start talking, and magically become connected. She had seen her sister do it all the time. People had tried and walk up to Julie, yet she could never shake a suspicion about their intention. It made her feel foreign inside her own body. Sex, luckily, had never been a problem. Julie found the act of seduction much less clouded and could easily become enchanted by a handsome stranger and sleep with him. There were less unpredictable factors and she knew what to control in the other. Not that she was sure of every outcome, but more often than not, Julie would forego any intimate relationship with a partner but still sleep with them. The purity of sex was a relief in the muddy concoctions of all other interaction in her life. It was the only place to find her vulnerability, if anyone had looked. But there was always something to do with sex, always a distraction to be found. It was almost impossible to say something out of the inability to sustain a silence.

"I have something to ask you." Julie pulled herself onto the kitchen counter next to Ben. "I've been thinking about my dreams recently. I can't seem to remember any of them. Do you remember any of your dreams?"

"Strange question." Ben smiled. "What does this have to do with anything?"

"You were the one talking about sensitivity!" Julie countered. "Do you remember your dreams, yes or not? I really don't. Isn't that strange? I mean, I can remember the ones I had as a kid, even now. But I can't remember any from the past ten years or so. Is that sad?" Julie took the mug that Ben held out to her. Eli stroked Ben's leg with his tail. The smell of peppermint filled in the kitchen, and Julie took a careful sip of her tea.

"Let me think …" Ben looked up. "Ah, yes, of course! I recently had one about my dad. We were in our family house in Haarlem. He was looking for something in the garden. I think there were some canyons and we had to find something buried in the earth. One of those strange dreams, I guess."

"Do you remember any details?"

"Hmm…not really. We were just looking for something. I remember feeling desperate. It was last weekend I had this one." He smiled proudly, opening his palms in emphasis, then continuing, "You know what I wonder? Since we are talking, I've always wondered why men are supposed to be less sensitive than women."

"Well, you don't have to," Julie answered, still trying to parry with one of her own dreams. "Does it bother you? You shouldn't care either way."

"I think you're just saying that. I think most people just say that. As if it was a fucking greeting card."

Julie leaned against the tiles and looked at Ben. He had a serious look, standing close enough to her to make her feel the distance.

"The whole business about being not caring." Ben was slightly agitated. "If I didn't care, then maybe I'd tell you that I want you to stay for longer. I would have to admit that I do like you, even though I can't tell you why. Not because I don't want to, but because I don't know myself.

I don't even know whether I like you that much, but I also don't want to be alone. So, there's that."

Eli had disappeared through the kitchen door. Julie stayed silent, raised her eyebrows and didn't move her eyes off of Ben. Although his point didn't surprise her, she wasn't sure how to react to the sudden nature of it. Meanwhile, the Dutchman lowered his head and started to take little steps to the left and then back, looking uncomfortable and grasping his mug tightly, crumbling his magnificent persona.

All Julie could think of was how people reacted to these declarations on reality TV. Slack-jawed, eyes peeling, the Julies of the show would stare at the orator while the camera panned to friends, all confirming how *crazy* the statement was. Having none of this at her disposal nor the inclination to drama, Julie was confronted with the duality of her casual relationship with Ben. The empty areas of his apartment were overwhelming, and she had no choice but to look at him while he kept eyes glued to the floor and stopped moving. Behind him, on the ground next to the entrance, Eli sat down, looking at them, reminding her that they weren't fully alone.

"I do care, Julie," Ben broke the silence with a half-whisper. "Everyone pretends not to care. They think that they forget their dreams. Whatever. It's the same thing, and it's a sickness. In reality, I think I might have had more of a chance not to care if you weren't here." He took a seat on one of the kitchen stools in front of Julie. "You just make it look so easy."

Julie could not help but smile. It was an impulsive smile she couldn't control, but there was also something charming in Ben's sudden shyness.

"Fair enough," she said.

Ben lifted his head.

"Fair enough. I'll stay with you a little longer."

"What? Really?" Ben seemed jumped and walked over to the counter. He gave her a passionate kiss and, in doing so, wrapped his arms around her back and picked her up to carry her back to bed. As he laid her down, he jumped in next to her and embraced her.

"I would like to care more, too," said Julie as she kissed him back. "I would like to care more. And remember my dreams."

Julie hid under the kitchen table, still angry with Margot for having called her mother. Margot sat on the corner of Julie's bed, her head sunk in her shoulders, pretending as if her guilt could do anything to help the situation. The minutes passed slowly in anticipation.

A new set of footsteps approached from the stairwell behind the door, followed by a double knock echoing through the studio. Julie arched her back at the sound of it. It was much louder than Margot's and her neighbor's knocks put together.

"Julie! It's me, dear! Margot told me you were home." Maman's voice sounded from the corridor.

How did she get here so quickly?

Julie had only a second to think about how to become invisible before Margot had sprung up to open the door. There was no time to do anything but freeze as she heard her mother step into the apartment. Noises and smells drifted through the kitchen from the little bedroom that Julie watched through a sliver of the kitchen door frame. Maman took off her coat and greeted Margot with two kisses. She was carrying her large black and white polka-dotted umbrella in one hand, matching her boots, and a loose leash in the other. That was when Julie connected the overwhelming stink with another living thing, Arnold. Her mother's gray-haired terrier trotted around Maman as she put her yellow sailor's coat down on the chaise longue. The dog's enthusiastic pitter-patter put Julie on high alert, and she hastened to higher ground in the corner of the kitchen's windowsill. She hoped he wouldn't see her or notice her scent from below.

Maman entered the kitchen. Without as much as lifting

her head or looking around, she began inspecting it and giving her personal comments to an invisible audience.

"Where are you, dear? Don't you want to say hello to your mother? When did you get a cat? Oh, it looks so dirty in here. You are just impossible…" Her words bounced around the tiled room. She did not seem to pay any attention to Julie at all, not even when she hissed.

"Maman, it's me," Julie uttered.

Maman looked up and around but didn't connect the voice to the animal. She seemed distracted by her own thoughts.

"Julie? Are you hiding somewhere?" she said, turning on the faucet.

"So, did you see, *madame*?" Margot said, joining into the kitchen.

"See what?" Maman asked.

Margot pointed at Julie, who spoke when her mother finally made eye contact with her. "Stop washing my dishes, goddammit."

Julie wasn't sure what type of reaction she expected of her mother. One of surprise would have been certainly normal, or maybe one of fear and helplessness, if she had to pick. However, her mother was never going to let her have this, a lifetime's supply of living in resentment and regret had trained her well to hide any vulnerability. Even though her eyes widened for a moment and she opened her mouth slightly, she managed to freeze her expression before she turned away. Just before Julie could detect a glimpse of panic in those dark eyes, Maman turned back to the running faucet. She turned it off.

"Well, Margot told me you were sick, but she didn't tell

me it was that bad! How did you manage to turn into a cat? And please, watch how you talk to your mother!" she added. Her voice trembled ever so slightly and she had to clear her throat.

"Did you have to bring that *thing*?" Julie looked over at Arnold. The dog had now picked up on Julie's smell but seemed to not have noticed her at the window. Running around the small studio, she could hear him sniffing every corner of her antique furniture.

"Arnold needed a walk. You'll have to excuse him. He is family, just like you. The little rascal got into the fountain at Anvers."

"Maman, I can't be having a dog here, now. I hate him."

"Now, now, Julie! Someone in your position shouldn't be spreading ill-wishes to others. He's done nothing wrong. I can't say the same thing about you." She looked at Julie for a second before wiping her forehead with the back of her palm and beginning to scrub a pot.

It hardly surprised Julie that her mother didn't directly address her transformation. Maman's active absence arose after years of dealing with her troubling daughters and the untimely abandonment by her husband. It was a mild way to describe that she hadn't been completely *there*. Five years ago, this mental state brought about the famed Arnold, who at least became an incentive for her to leave the house more often, which she used to dread. The two became connected at the hip and the cause of many arguments about parts of her life that Maman could control less than her dog. Other matters that had already moved to the side years prior became forgotten. Before long, in her own little transformation, Maman had turned into that old lady with a terrier.

Telling to what extent dogs mimic their owners, Arnold had mildly ignored Julie for most of his life. Anya joked that it may have been a side effect of unconditional love, yet Julie felt that Arnold enjoyed their meetings even less than her. There was unresolved jealousy in their mutual tug and pull for attention from Maman that neither was ready to overcome.

It would be wrong to say that Maman's detachment sprang out of mere depression. Long before her husband left, Maman had always described herself as a listless romantic. She was much more outspoken and outgoing than her husband. Julie knew that she had once been very idealistic and stood for what she believed. After all, her parents had never liked the man she married, but that never stopped her from standing by him, even after she was proven wrong. She was stubborn. That may have been the easiest way to put it. If it weren't for her flashes of empathy and that softened her face every once in a while, you would have even believed the act. Her ego had started to fade with time, likely to do with the inadvertent tranquility of her advancing age. Julie was hoping for one of those flashes to be present that day.

Throughout her short-lived attempts for a new romantic connection, Julie's mother had forgotten to exist in the present. No one stayed around for longer than a breakfast coffee or an early dinner. And even though the clear revelation hadn't made her complacent, she had never dealt with the passing of her past self and the irrational ideas that had once made her who she wanted to be.

A strange sound came from outside. Both Arnold and

Julie were the first to react. While Arnold gave off a bark and ran into the bedroom, Julie lifted her head to look out of the window, a dividing line of intelligence from the canine. He didn't recognize the sound of a distant flute being christened by an amateur player. Julie couldn't see the player but imagined it had to be the little girl from the second floor, whom she had seen walk through the courtyard with her rectangular case. The flute resonated up through the courtyard dancing off of the thin windows around the top floors for a few breaths.

"Julie, I won't make a big deal out of this." Maman's voice cut through the music. "I cleaned up this time, but you should really keep the kitchen in a better way. You know that the bacteria that build up in a sink can literally kill you!"

"Can they turn you into a cat?" Julie sneered.

"We'll come to that in a second." Maman put a hand on her hip and looked for a place to sit down. She took the chair closest to Julie and started inspecting her.

"What?" Julie didn't like this attention.

"I could think of a few reasons why this happened to you." Maman smacked the outside of her thigh. "Did you remember to wish Grandpa Philippe a happy birthday?"

Maman rambled on. "Last year, when I was visiting your auntie Danielle out in Limousin—you remember her, right? She told me that when her husband wouldn't agree to see Mami Lou, he became like a frog. His appetite changed, and he only ate flies for a week! So, it does happen! Maybe it's a family curse?"

"But I did call Grandpa."

"Well … then, maybe it was somebody else?"

66

Julie rolled to her side. "Maman, please stop. I asked Margot to take me to Monceau. I just want to go outside. And I would like to go while it's still sunny."

"I wouldn't be so demanding in your situation! Think of what part of the universe you might have upset to turn out like this. You're in no position to make demands!"

"Maman, I haven't upset anyone. On top of that, I don't feel like I am getting punished by anyone except you. How did you get here so quickly, anyway?"

Maman looked flustered by Julie's question and stood up demonstratively. "Well, *mademoiselle*. If you must know, I was in the neighborhood when Margot called me, coming out of my classes at Chateau-Rouge!"

Arnold noticed that his owner had focused on something on the counter. He couldn't see Julie but was making a lot of noise by running back and forth underneath the window. Julie did not indulge him and stayed covered, elongated by the window. Her mother walked back to the entrance, passing Margot, who was standing silently in the door frame of the kitchen. Maman came back with her purse and a face full of excitement that looked completely out of place.

"I want you to be honest with me, all right? Margot, you too!"

Margot nodded without saying a word.

"Look Julie, cat or no cat. You know, Arnold and I have been through so much," Maman began. "All this walking around and not knowing what to do. And so I said, no more! We needed something new, something new to look forward to. We didn't want to keep lingering about waiting for it to hit us - we went out and found it! Something for the hands. And to relax the mind. Wanted to get as far away from these thoughts about your father as possible. And to be closer to you and your sister. Together with my little Arnold!" She squatted down to pet him. He calmed down and laid down flat on his back next to her feet. Maman pulled out a purple leaflet from her purse.

"We've decided to make time!" she exclaimed, reaching the leaflet to Julie. "You can still read, right?"

Julie perked herself up, not sure if she heard correctly. She looked down at the leaflet that her mother held a few inches away from her nose. *'Become a master clockmaker.'* Julie had to read it a few times over, keeping her head locked in position. She had absolutely nothing to say, as Maman stuffed the silence. Margot, lured by curiosity, had walked over to Julie to look at the leaflet as well.

"You see, Julie," Maman continued. "I was always so afraid of having too much time that I forgot to realize that it's up to me to make it count. Time is such a precious little thing in the end. And we do have so little of it! I was too desperate for it to move quicker, and now, all I wish for is for it to come back! I need to live in this time that we have in our hands. So…there I went!" Maman put the leaflet down in front of Julie and took a breath, finally.

"I feel I've always had a fascination with old watches and clocks. And I've just come back from my first class and have to say that I love it! We've been reading a lot about these old clock masters and their secret traits. It's fascinating, you know? I wish I could tell you about all of those amazing secrets, Julie, but I can't … there is a covenant."

Julie looked up at Margot, who was still standing in front of her. A seagull jumped across the roof and caught her attention. Gladly. Her mother continued without dismay, now seeking the attention of Margot, who had not looked up from the leaflet.

"You know what?" said Maman. "It's alright if I tell you one of them! I'm sure they wouldn't mind anyway, just one. You see, these masters, they sometimes make these little engravings on golden sundials, written in Latin. One of my favorites that we saw today says '*Serius es quam cogitas.*'" Maman drew a sign into the air. "You know what it means?"

Margot looked up to listen to the answer. Maman looked straight at her. "It means '*it's later than you think*'. Isn't that brilliant?"

Julie looked at Maman gleaming around the room, oblivious to the lack of enthusiasm in everyone except Arnold. The terrier was wiggling his tail at full force, hearing the excitement in his owner's voice. Maman bent down again and gave him another belly rub.

"Arnold loves it," Maman resolved.

"Madame Galles?" Margot spoke softly, to the great relief of Julie.

Maman either didn't hear her or pretended not to. She changed topic.

"When will I finally see you with a young man these days?" said her mom. "Doesn't matter if you're a cat. Don't look away! Look at your little sister. I mean, she isn't a prime example on all things, but at least I see her with her boyfriends."

"Margot, you were going to say something to my mother?" Julie turned to her friend. The clock making topic had blown over quicker than expected. It may have been another advantage in being a cat: acting as a showstopper in other people's absurdity.

"*Madame* … what are we going to do about Julie?" Margot spoke slowly.

"What do you want me to do? It's hopeless," Maman replied, still flustered from her monologue.

"No, I mean, her … I mean, her transformation?!" Margot pointed to Julie.

"Yes, I know." Maman calmed her voice, taking a breath and looking at her cat daughter.

"If you must talk about this, could you at least do it without me?" Julie interrupted. She was tired of being part of pointless discussions. "Go to the bedroom or even outside. I don't want to hear it, just take me to the park like you promised."

"*Disce dies numerare tuos, my dear.*" Maman pointed a finger in the air. "Learn to value your days."

"Oh, please, Maman."

"Alright, Margot, let's go outside like she wants."

With these words, Maman gestured Margot to follow her out of the kitchen and out of the studio. Arnold followed without hesitation. As soon as the door closed behind them, Julie felt the room's silence cover her like a silk sheet. This collection of energies departed, and she closed her eyes to appreciate it fully. The flutist picked up her volume again and allowed the new cat to drift into a daydream in *Amazing Grace*.

Anya wouldn't have hesitated to take Julie out of Paris. Maman's appearance at her doorstep and the perpetual delay made Julie wish for her sister to be there more than ever. Anya was always up for adventure, a quality that was at least half-responsible for Maman's mental state. Whatever the intensity of Maman's opinion about anything, she never let all her worry go to Julie. It only seemed like the older sibling received more scrutiny due to the whimsical nature of her missteps. Whimsical, in comparison to the hurricane of trouble that was her younger sister.

Anya would have been best described as a proud mess-up and amateur revolutionary. This in itself wouldn't have been that much of a problem, if it wasn't for her devilish seduction of others, first and foremost Julie.

Julie often wondered if the two had come from the same two parents. Both sisters were only a year apart in age and had been educated identically, yet, somehow, ended up as different as the witches of Oz. Julie was working for a namely corporation, and the few friends she had were a result of her immediate surroundings. Just like Margot, they were all lovingly predictable, cocooning her in a stable tranquility. On the other side, Anya had amassed her occasionally employed and eclectic group of friends through wild parties and was plotting nothing less than a *coup d'état* every other weekend. Anya's friends were rowdy, and all of them callously careless with their critique of modern society. It had made Anya visibly sadistic toward people's reactions. Julie was never sure if her sister really meant what she said or even knew what she was talking about. Her ideas seemed in good spirits but all over the place and made it hard for Julie to understand what her sister was actually fighting for.

Still, Julie rarely interrupted her feisty ambitions because they were usually entertaining.

Maman had strong opinions about what she called "Anya's excesses". In her, Maman saw a spirit of her own destructive youth, causing a mixture of worried and jealous feelings and leading to many hurtful arguments with her daughter. Julie avoided these arguments to the best of her ability as they became repetitive over the years. Anya would make anything a case for resistance, and then Maman would escalate it to a matter of discipline. It could have been as simple a matter as when Maman asked her to run down to the bakery for breakfast croissants. Anya would refuse, arguing against the Maman's obsession with white bread pastry and Maman telling her to better listen, or else. It ruined the croissants and the breakfast altogether.

When she was ten, Anya argued with a family friend for hours about depictions of French colonialists on postal stamps. Their father used to say her bitter distrust and passion came from all the licorice she ate. One of his seemingly unconcerned quips that hid even his deeper concern for his daughter's idealism.

By age twelve, Anya would no longer be convinced of anything by her mother, and only their father was able to sway Anya to act. If the two were spent in yet another bitter fight, he would intervene with his calming voice, playing it off as if there was no fundamental difference between the two. It didn't help, but Julie knew he felt his duty in it. If the fights between Maman and Anya carried any results at all, it was that they left Julie out of Maman's spotlight.

Through all this, the sisters stayed inseparable no matter how different they were. Anya never made Julie feel bad about her calmer relationship with their parents while Julie remained the most imminent confessor of her sister's vices. She knew that Anya hid a profound empathy behind her veil of critique and resistance. It was her spirit that was unhappy with leading a stressless life. The tranquility that Julie longed for was a prospect that depressed Anya more than anything. She once described herself as a bad gambler upset at a winning table. Anya wished for a more romantic procession of everyone's life. In the same way that Julie never wished for greatness, Anya wanted a great battle in her life. A conquest of some demon to eventually grant her not only reason but also legitimacy. She got involved with anything to help her hunt for this sensation, from animal rights to underground raves. When Anya talked with Julie, she was always full of fire for some new cause, not unlike Maman.

Two months before the day of her transformation, Anya had called Julie to the little café *Au Petit Poucet* on the top *Rue Blanche* after work. She sounded excited on the phone.

"Victor is very nice, you'll see. I won't forgive you if you don't join!" she said, leaning over the little table between them.

"You've just met the guy. And he is inviting you to the catacombs? Don't you think it's a bit strange?" Julie took a sip from her hot cocoa. Anya had already spit out a story about a new guy that she was seeing as they were ordering at the bar.

"It's just a thing that they do. Isn't it great?! I said you'll come, too, obviously!" Anya smiled.

Julie knew better than to keep resisting her sister's request. Of all the ideas Anya had thrown at her, at least this one didn't involve any party or marching with people. Although Julie enjoyed listening to her sister trying to convince her, it was these two points that made a difference. Aided by the soothing aroma of the gifted hot cocoa.

Only a week and a half later, Julie found herself alongside Anya and her more-than-friends Victor inside the tunnels of the Parisian catacombs. They had been walking below ground for about thirty minutes and were standing in front of a point in the path that was almost entirely flooded. There were only about four feet of air left between the surface of the water and the ceiling of the tunnel.

"So, what do you think of him?" Anya whispered to her sister. The tunnel made her quiet words sound like a creeping insect. Julie was more interested in how they would proceed.

"Wait! Victor? Is there a way around the water?" Julie asked their leader, walking ahead. She was horrified to see Victor keeping steady without hesitation.

Anya turned to Julie, adjusting her headlamp to point at the ceiling. She did not say anything but gave Julie a commanding look. Julie nodded in understanding and tried to think positively.

"Some paths are flooded, but it is just sedimentary water," Victor explained as he was first to enter the muddy water. "It's completely harmless. Just a little cold." He spoke calmly, without turning around.

"I guess he's your type," Julie whispered back to Anya. Anya smiled back.

On one hand, Julie had envied Anya for trusting someone so blindly. On the other, she was worried about seeing Anya ending up in these situations forever. Wading through muddy water, or hanging off of rock walls, or, god forbid, in a political campaign. She seemed insatiable in her search for adventure and someone to do it with.

Victor didn't share the physical characteristics of Anya's typical love interests. He had a slender figure, making him seem boyish and a little undernourished. His dark hair fell to his shoulders behind which he hid half of his face at all time. He wasn't very talkative and had been giving elusive answers that found a highlight in his description of the water. He hadn't been very clear as to how long their trip would take or where they were going. Still, he did not seem menacing, Julie felt, simply in his own world.

"I heard you say cataphile before. What does that mean, exactly?" Julie asked him as they got back to dry land. The three of them had waddled through the ice-cold water for a few minutes and kept on without taking a break.

"The cataphiles make sure the catacombs stay safe," he answered through his hair, turning around to Julie. "We develop them. It comes from the words *cata*, short for catacombs, and the *phil*, for the ancient Greek for loving." His voice carried soothingly through the tunnel.

"Does it ever get dangerous down here?" Julie caught up to him.

"Which part? The exploring?"

"The water, the illegality. I mean, what happens if you get hurt down here?"

"Well, if something happens…nothing happens. You're done. That is why I wouldn't recommend going by yourself. People do get lost from time to time."

"Luckily, we have the best guide with us!" Anya interjected, walking closely behind them.

"Aren't we lucky." Julie stopped the interrogation for that moment. As much as she grew accustomed to Victor's strange nature, she did not feel as confident about their leader as Anya.

Being a big sister felt like a burden sometimes. Julie felt the responsibility of watching over Anya, even though she didn't feel qualified in the slightest. After all, all she had going for herself were similarly unfounded and doomed relationships.

Julie kept quiet for the rest of the journey. She did not want to seem confident enough to be left behind. They passed a dozen crossroads and took many turns. It was certain that without Victor, they would not find their way back.

From time to time, after walking for what felt like hours, the limestone-carved corridors got wider. As they advanced, there appeared to be more crossings and wider rooms interrupting the dull perpetuity of tunnels. The smell was neutral, almost clinical, and the surfaces of the floor and the walls were surprisingly smooth. Carvings of names and dates and colorful graffiti adorned some of them. Julie tried to imagine the people who liked to hide in these underground souks. On one occasion, Victor stopped to show them an engraving on the wall. A small group of the French Resistance had made it in 1943, he explained. It had tried to infiltrate the Gestapo's seat at *Denfert-Rochereau* that year.

"Looks like my friends are already here." Victor pointed ahead.

Julie gave Anya a look of confusion. It was the first time Victor had mentioned anything about meeting anyone.

Throughout their descent, they had not crossed a soul, the engravings being the only sign of other humans there. Julie looked ahead and saw a dim light.

The trio entered a grandiose room spotted with limestone columns sprayed over by layers of graffiti. The only source of light ahead of them was the small fire from a burner sitting atop a limestone carved table with two people sitting on an equally carved bench. Julie halted to observe this surreal sight from afar. The smell of the Bunsen burner filled the room of this underworld. Anya followed Victor to the private circle around the table. Julie followed with a delay and usual hesitation when she was called to meet the seated strangers.

"Julie, come over here to say hello!" Anya yelled, already sitting at the table with them.

"As we are in the catacombs, you have to get used to people using their cata-names," Victor explained to Julie, who sat down next to her sister.

"What is your cata-name, Victor? Let me guess… something, like Frederic?" asked Anya, turning to him.

"No, no," he mumbled.

"All cata-names are rooted in mythology," the girl said at the table. A short blonde haircut, she was wearing an oversized black hoodie, worn-out jeans, and rubber boots. She seemed to observe her surroundings sharply and spread a witty aura around her.

"His name is Bacchus."

Victor moved a strain of hair out of his face.

"Normally, it would have to start with the first letter of your first name, but there are only a few choices for a guy with the letter V. All I get is Virgo or Venus. So, I went with

Bacchus instead. A sort of Spanish V."

Julie saw him smile for the first time since they met. He turned to his two friends and introduced them to Anya and Julie.

"These are my friends Syrene, the maniac, and Cyclopse, the genius. Syrene, Cyclopse, meet Anya and her sister Julie."

"Epic introduction, Bacchus." Syrene laughed. "Welcome, sisters!"

She got up, followed by Cyclopse, to greet both newcomers with two kisses and a warm smile.

"We use these names down here because we aren't the same down here as we are up there," Syrene said and pointed up. "It would not make sense for us to use the same names." She winked at Julie.

Cyclopse, the thin young guy to her right, resembled Victor, except that his shoulder-length hair was curly. His immediate distinctive feature, however, was a black pirate hat he wore with one white feather sticking out over his left ear. He did not seem to mind or even notice who presently joined his table. Julie judged that out of the two, Syrene was the one to listen to.

"It took me getting under the city to understand what is happening up there," Syrene said.

"Yes, and now, we like it down here, more than up there," Cyclopse added, revealing a big yellow-toothed smile.

Julie sat directly across from the two mythological namesakes, distantly amused by their introduction. Whether out of fear of being left alone or hesitation to make a smart comment, she smiled back.

"It's not like we seek glory down here," Syrene continued. "When you become a cataphile, your main objective is the camaraderie you find underground. And the survival of the catacombs." She moved up to the table and shaped her hands to touch both her index fingers and thumbs together. "We observe simple rules to maintain the balance here. Don't disrespect, be inclusive, and help out…simple stuff. Other than that, you could say or do anything you wish. We do not have a gate or barrier; anyone is welcome to join if they are willing to sacrifice for this place."

"Sacrifice?" Anya asked.

"You must be ready to sacrifice the part of your life aboveground and have it only become one of the two lives you lead." Syrene smiled.

"Is that why you are here?" Anya asked. "Because you were tired of your aboveground life?"

"We were tired of dealing with an economy of takers. Everyone just takes, takes, takes… Here, we give," Cyclopse intervened. "Up there, I work in an office. They take my minutes, and I pay my taxes and answer to my boss. Then I come down here and can live the life I actually want."

"So, you're hiding?" Anya asked. Victor shifted uncomfortably while Julie remained silent.

Syrene snickered.

Julie was waiting for Anya to make one of her famous comments. She recognized her teasing tone but was too scared to be left 40 feet under the streets of Paris to comment.

"Anya, maybe not now?" Julie reached for her sister's arm.

The energy of the room became charged. Even Victor, who until now had only participated in the conversation with the odd nod, was looking at Anya. She, however, remained unfazed, looking straight at Syrene. There was no indication of her dismissing the question or moving on to another topic. Julie could feel Syrene's challenge through the sides of her eyes. It was quiet until Anya continued.

"I don't want to be rude, I'm just curious. Don't you see the contradiction in what you're saying? You want to control your own life, right? Cyclopse, you said that you only live your actual life down here. So, what do you lead up there?"

Syrene didn't allow Cyclopse to answer.

"What you seem to assume, Anya, is that there needs to be a meaning to what we do here." Syrene leaned back, and her voice sounded surprisingly calm, which relaxed Julie. "We don't think about it as much as you. To me, being a cataphile isn't an escape from my aboveground problems. I lead two lives because that is what makes me happy. One enables the other. I speak for all of us when I say that being down here doesn't make sense. It has no intrinsic meaning. But isn't that also the case for your life aboveground?

There are people who come down here and find nothing. They hoped to find it as obvious as it is aboveground. They need to see an economic gain, a generated income, or a bigger house, car, or family. Those are the same people you can never trust with something that matters to you, but not to them. A work of art, for example. Because that is what we do in the end - we live in an art piece of ourselves. There, society decided that this is not a way to live, so we had to find a place to escape. As you put it."

"You live in a piece of art?" Anya questioned.

"In a way, yes, of course! What else could it be? We made it with our own hands. We can feel its power!" Syrene smiled. She saw that her calm explanation had transfixed the two sisters.

Julie realized that this must not have been the first time she was making this speech. Well-versed and spoken, it was. She was slightly convinced indeed.

"We follow our heart," Syrene continued. "Have you read one of those quotes they write on the walls in Montmartre? It goes, 'Love runs these streets.' That was us - we've written them. But they weren't for Montmartre, they were for down here! Love runs these catacombs! Where would we be without love for what we do? This table, you—"

"That's silly," Julie interrupted her, barely believing that she did.

Syrene stopped talking and looked at her. Their looks met, and Julie felt embarrassed, as the entire cave turned to her in expectation. It was Syrene's calm glance that took away her anxiety for her to continue.

"Don't you find that dangerous?" Julie asked quietly into the round. "You know… to let love guide you?"

"No, not at all," Syrene replied, raising her eyebrows. "Isn't it the most wonderful thing we can do as humans? What would you rather do? Close yourself from the world?"

Julie didn't want to reply. She looked into Syrene's eyes, flickering in the shadows of the central flame. She could feel how different they were from each other, even if they spoke the same language. It was as if they were completely different beings. This wasn't her home. Anya poured a glass of red wine and gestured to everyone if they wanted any. Cyclopse and Syrene nodded. Julie continued to speak to the sound of wine being poured.

"With love, you start to have expectations. All your insecurities come to light and feel exposed."

Julie was happy that Anya was sitting next to her. She was having a difficult enough time speaking up in front of everyone.

"Someone's just gone through a tough break-up, haven' they?" Syrene said with a smile. "Look, I don't want you to think that I am trying to convince you. If you feel like your way has brought you happiness, who am I to talk? But let me ask you this: How would you ever convince yourself to do anything without real passion? If you're never willing to take a leap of faith ... I don't know how I'd function."

"She just hides it," Anya said. "She's more passionate than all of us put together." Julie reached over the table and poured herself a glass of wine, too, embarrassed by her sister's words.

"Then you're not too different from my friend here." Syrene put her arm around Cyclopse and made a welcoming gesture to the table. "Quiet worlds."

"Let's drink to love, no matter what form it takes," Victor said.

Syrene laughed again and added, "To your heart being wrong sometimes and right all other times. As long as you live."

Julie nodded.

Anya poured three more glasses and reached her cup to the middle for a cheer.

"To the catacombes!" she sang.

"To the catas!" The rest responded, their glasses clinking together over the limestone table.

Margot and Maman had walked out into the hallway to talk. Julie heard Maman's boots squeak away from the door and then a mumbled conversation commenced behind the wall.

The melody from her downstairs friend, some distant honking, and the rumbling voices settled in the space around the windowsill. Julie squinted her eyes and tried to see if anything changed by staring at a spot on the other side of the kitchen. The light dimmed around her pupils and she felt the weight of her head pulling her down to her furry arms. Images started to reel behind her eyelids at once. There were chases through a town and faces of panic in anyone she recognized, her baker and her grandmother. They pointed to a gate in the back that burst open as soon as she saw it. Julie had to run from the flood. Through narrow streets with the water at her heels, until she arrived at an open field where it all sank into the earth. The field was purple up to the horizon. Lavender filled the air, a pinching tingle in her nose.

Julie woke up with an uneasy feeling. There was something scary awaiting her that she didn't feel like exploring further. She turned her curiosity back to the reality outside her door instead. The chatter had become agitated and practically invited eavesdropping.

Julie squeezed through the half-opened window to slide onto the railing outside her kitchen. There was an instant relief to be in the open air and surprisingly little fear for standing on the ledge of the 6th floor. With close to no effort, Julie hopped across the slanted rooftop to arrive at the ceiling hatch that opened over the hallway leading to her studio. She peeked her head inside and saw her mother standing directly below it, shoulder to shoulder with Margot, about ten feet away from the apartment door.

"Please, stop saying that!" Margot said, standing in a tense position while Maman leaned into her.

"Now, hold on! Once again, let me tell you…" Maman exhaled.

She put an arm on Margot's shoulder and frowned. Arnold was trotting around happily, sniffing along the corners of the hall.

What a happy knob.

"Better?" Maman continued serenely.

"No, not really," replied Margot. "I want to know what is happening, and you are talking about something completely different. It's as if you don't care about what happened to Julie. It's too much to be a friend right now."

Maman made an impatient move at Margot's last sentence. She took a step away from Margot and grabbed a pack of cigarettes out of her coat's pocket. Her movements were fidgety and she had trouble keeping the fire to the tip of her thin *Gauloise*. She took one long drag, looking down the narrowing end of the hall and proceeded to squeeze the stub at the wall with force. The giant cloud she blew out Julie had to dodge as it rose up.

"It's always the same," Maman said.

Her voice was low. She took three more steps away from Margot, mumbling to herself and twisting the pack in her pocket that made a crunching sound. She made the incoherent impression of a mental patient trying to readjust, while Margot stared at her helplessly. The seconds flew by at half their normal pace, waiting for anything to shake the frozen painting. Julie thought of jumping through the hatch to diffuse the standstill herself, but her mother beat her to it.

"Oh dear," she said quietly, letting out a sigh and smiling at Margot.

"Madame? Are you OK?" Margot asked.

Maman shifted her weight from one leg to the other and looked to pick up more energy with each breath. "Well, there's nothing to say." "I suppose you are right, let's get back to Julie and get through the day." She scratched the back for her head. "Just one thing. Don't you think that… ah, never mind."

"How I wish it was all a dream." Margot returned to her own broken record.

"Now, now. Let's not get apocalyptical." Maman strengthened her tone and returned to wrapping one arm around Margot, but it was too late.

It had become Margot's time to be on edge. With an arm lying around her shoulders, Julie could hear the muffled sound of her friend sobbing. A few irregular breaths through a dam of held back tears that would no longer be held back. Maman pulled her closer.

The scene had momentarily lost Julie's interest, who pulled her head back away from the hatch and laid down on the warm dark gray roof tiles. The sun tickled her skin that was ruffled by the wind flying over the rooftops. It was a perfect day to stay outside, and Julie was tired of the unnecessary delays. This was supposed to be her day of action, and yet she had only been witness to the woes of others. There was a pull in her gut that made her feel nauseous as if she was right to be ignored. If society had only personal wars left to fight in, no one seemed keen to declare hers the one to step into. It made Julie think of how violently she saw her mother extinguish her cigarette, something she had never seen her do. There'd been occasions that her mother would sneak away for a cigarette, to the family car or balcony, even if neither parent admitted to it. But she'd never seen Maman so fidgety, so at a loss and at a need. It was as if she had seen beyond the mirror that she had sworn to her entire life. Julie wondered about all those other moments she had never seen, fleeting instances which the child was never shown. Perhaps because the parents don't want them to, or perhaps the young ones didn't recognize them. It was a shame that she never thought about it or simply ignored any suspicion. Maybe her mother wouldn't have been as foreign to her as she had always assumed. Julie looked back down into the hall.

Maman had picked up a phone and was dialing someone.

"Go make sure that she doesn't run away. I'll be right in," she said to Margot, who was already halfway back to the studio.

Julie sprinted back down to her ledge outside of her kitchen window. She jumped inside, barely touching the frame and landed on the tiled floor between the sink and the table. The door opened and Julie heard Margot take one more deep breath with Maman talking on the phone in the distance. She had just enough time to wonder who she was calling.

Margot walked into the kitchen. "There you are! Hiding? You are too much like a cat already. It's scary."

"What's going on? Are we going to Monceau? Have you decided?" Julie asked.

"We're trying to solve your condition."

"My condition?"

"Yes, to see how we can turn you back into a human."

"Wait. You promised me we'd go to the park." Julie hadn't even thought about turning back to human.

"Don't you want to be you again?" Margot sounded desperate.

"Margot, why don't you let me worry about that."

"Why do you have to be like this, Julie? I'm just trying to help you."

"I am telling you that I feel fine and just want to get out. I'm not asking for anything else!" Julie meowed in aggravation.

Margot lifted her eyebrow as if it proved her point.

"I feel like I'm talking to a wall," Julie said.

Maman came back into the studio and Julie waited for her to join them in the kitchen. Julie jumped back onto the windowsill at the smell of the dog. Maman didn't pay any attention to Margot's raised expression and walked right over to her ginger daughter cat. She pulled up a chair from the other side of the table by the window and sat in front of Julie. She gestured for Margot to stay with Arnold, who had been getting increasingly agitated with the smell of movement in the air.

"Julie, what do you want to do? I have my second orientation class starting in two hours, so I can only take care of you until around 7 p.m. I called your sister, who will join us later and spend the rest of the day with you. I can't miss this session, I'm sure you understand. Then we'll meet later and discuss this as a family."

Julie's heart jumped at the mention of Anya.

"Of course, Maman. As I said to Margot, I just want to

go to Monceau," she replied in the tone of pure obedience.

"Well, it's only four metro stops away," Maman said. "I'll come along for some fresh air, but we can't take Arnold along. Margot?"

No one had noticed, but Margot was now holding her phone out in front of her and looked to be recording the conversation between Maman and Julie.

"Margot!" Maman screamed. "What in the world are you doing?"

"I'm just…I mean…just a short…video…"

"This isn't your everyday gossip. Hand me that phone!" Maman got up and snatched the phone out of Margot's hand.

Arnold, sensing the tension peak again, started barking, and Maman tried to calm him with her free hand. Margot collapsed into a kitchen chair, just as miserably as she had earlier. Julie laid down on her side and watched the interaction with bemusement. Margot had positively surprised her with her act, even if it seemed to have taken a toll on her.

"I can't believe you call yourself Julie's friend! How shameful!" Maman clamored at a visibly scared Margot. Arnold continued barking. Maman continued talking. "It's decided. You are taking a break from today. Truly too much. You'll go and take Arnold for a walk until I call you! I will take my daughter to the park alone. Right now, please, before I lose it, too!"

Hanging her head in embarrassment, Margot nodded, got up, and picked up the leash that Maman handed her without any objection. Arnold would not stop barking. Maman pointed them toward the exit and gave Arnold one more pet before pushing them outside. Margot didn't have time to look back inside.

"Just keep walking until I call you. Don't let him eat anything off the street," Maman yelled through the door. Julie heard Margot's footsteps dim toward the stairwell, accompanied by the smell of another freshly lit cigarette.

Maman walked into Julie's bedroom without losing any time. She brought out Julie's brown leather bag and started to pack. Julie was still celebrating the exit of Arnold's yapping when she turned her attention to her paws, licking off the dirt that they had collected on the roof. She would stop every few licks and lift her head to watch Maman packing some cookies and blankets for their excursion. Julie was getting excited, until the moment Maman reached for her to put her in the bag as well.

"Let me put you in," said Maman as she reached for Julie. She had put the bag on the table in front of her daughter and reached down before receiving a reply. Julie hissed at her mother and struck her left hand with her paw.

"Julie! What? What now?" Maman screamed, pulling her arm back. "Do you want to go, or not?"

Mother and daughter looked at each other. Julie decided to play it off as if nothing happened. Her mother waited, mending her cut.

"Look, we can't just walk out of the house like this," she spoke, holding her hand under the faucet.

"I'll get in myself. Just put the bag on the floor," said Julie.

"What a princess! Right... here," Maman did as told, and Julie climbed in the bag.

The pair walked out of the building, turning right toward

Place de Pigalle. Maman carried the bag on her shoulder and had not said a word since they left the studio. Julie understood that through their silence, they had both agreed to attract as little attention to their party as possible. That included avoiding any prolonged public conversations between a human and a cat.

Julie peaked her head out of the bag and rejoiced in being finally on her way. She knew that if she was lucky, she might have been able to spot a few cats on their walk. After the initial scare of seeing one of her new kin, she was carrying unbridled excitement in the thought of meeting a fellow feline. She was eager to see whether cats—as a cat—would be less annoying than humans had been so far. She had a hunch.

The streets were packed with all sorts of people. Julie didn't recognize her usual businessmen or fish vendors she crossed on her morning slaloms to work. The atmosphere seemed much more in the moment and relaxed. The formal clothes had been replaced by colorful outfits of delivery men and families with matching "I love Paris" t-shirts. It was endearing to see this new grouping. Julie imagined the groups, waiting one behind the other around the corners of buildings to relay at the strike of some predetermined hour. Once the clock struck 9:00 am and the businessmen had been off the street, the delivery men took over, then came the tourists, only to be replaced by the businessmen's return formation at 6:00 pm. Maman and Julie had to be careful not to appear too out of place, but no one made eye contact. Much to Julie's disappointment, the cat that usually sat in the alley next to *Folies Pigalle* wasn't there either and Maman kept marching on.

Walking up the metro stop, the two had nearly completed their first leg, when a loud "Madame Galles?" made Maman stop mid-step. Julie could have recognized the smoky voice from miles away but had least expected it in this surrounding. It stood out impressively. As Maman had stopped and turned around slowly, Julie could already see Mathilde was catching up to them in an unsightly trot. She was holding one arm down to keep her red summer dress from flying up.

"Madame Galles, I thought that it was you! How have you been? Did you just come from Julie's?"

"I...I...Hello...I, hello," Maman stammered. She reached for the fresh wound on her hand from her daughter's strike and started scratching.

"I was just thinking of going by myself. You see, we had an incident at the Galleries and she hasn't been replying. Bad coincidence, I am sure, but I must have her help me at once. Couldn't wait for her much longer." Mathilde spoke by overlooking the confusion on Maman's face.

"Oh...really? Well, I must say, you know." Maman tried to reply.

"Did you see her?"

"Well, yes, but no." Maman was trying hard. "She's not well, you should know. Caught a terrible fever, I'm afraid."

"Oh no!" Mathilde screamed. A few passersby turned around. "No, it can't be! I mean, poor thing, of course, and with this weather! How on earth? Well, I must go by and bring her something."

"That won't be necessary, really," Maman interrupted. "She's about to go to the doctor."

"Great! I'll accompany her."

"No, I mean…the doctor is coming to her."

"I'll wait, no problem."

"She's all tired now, really. You mustn't insist." Maman's voice had gotten progressively stricter and surer. Mathilde was starting to notice a matter of mystery in her words and took a moment to scan Maman. Julie tried to hide her head further down in the bag, but it was too late.

"What do you have here?" asked Mathilde.

"A cat I am taking care of for a friend," Maman replied briskly and took half a step around.

"She's very cute." Mathilde reached out to give Julie a pat, but Maman jerked the bag away.

"Yes, yes, just a bit demanding," said Maman. "Now, if you will excuse me, I have to press on. Please don't bother with seeing Julie. Hopefully she will be back on her feet by tomorrow." Maman turned her back and made her way to the top of the stairs to the metro.

"Oh right…you're sure I shouldn't go see her? Maybe I can help with something?" Mathilde repeated her question from a distance.

"I wouldn't even try if I were you. I wouldn't be surprised if she doesn't even hear the door."

Maman sprinted down the steps with those words, raising her left hand without turning around to wave goodbye. Julie felt the grip on the bag. A loud "Bye!" followed them down to the metro's hallway. Maman continued through the underground gate, making sure that the till worker didn't see the cat and arrived at the platform, both relieved to have escaped the situation quickly. Julie felt something like pride in her mother and let out a quiet "Thanks."

Julie would have commonly seen *Parc Monceau* on exactly two occasions: the odd weekend morning when she would motivate herself for a jog or an all too seldom solo picnic with a book. Either way, she had always been under the impression of never visiting it enough. Although the park was only four metro stops away, it existed in another world, within the city limits of Paris but out of its reach. There was something in the air that put the earth and wilderness in starker contrast to everything around it. Julie was sure there were symphonies written about it by people who had never stepped inside its microcosms.

Monceau's charm also lay in the hands of its international flair, being surrounded by 25 of the most grandiose embassies of the city. Taking a break from sitting inside their fine buildings, well-dressed diplomats would often be seen zipping across the park's footpaths. Each of their delegations had, at some point, gifted the keeper of the park one of their country's native plants, resulting in an ever-evolving, foolishly diverse flora. Japanese Sakura blossoming next to an ancient Lebanese Cedar and the aromatic Greek olives, while the Spanish councils and German financiers discussed worldly matters in their shade. Julie had found it a good sport to spot these dignitaries among the local visitors. Their groupings had a notable lack of blankets or picnic baskets that made them stand out from the rest of the parkgoers. If time was the currency of Monceau, the average Parisian knew to spend it slowly, while the foreigners spent it carelessly, involved in a deep conversation with a companion or their phone.

Two primary schools bordered the park: *St. Eustache*, an all-boys Catholic school by the southern entrance of *Rue*

Lisbonne, and *École Theodore Herzl*, a mixed Jewish school on the western gate looking at *Avenue Hoche*. Both had programs that took place in the park after classes, which meant that floods of screeching pupils filled its lawns each afternoon. Were it not for the presence of girls at École Herzl, Julie would have also had to make it a game to guess which pupil belonged to which school as all the boys wore black pants with white button-down shirts. It seemed a common denominator of schools of all confessions to be cruel to children in that way.

The deep green benches of Monceau would be alternately occupied by old couples sitting quietly and young couples smooching. Forming a long loop around the oval shape of the park, the main footpath was the triumphant promenade route through the park. On it mothers pushed their buggies, teenagers stirred trouble, diplomats and businesspeople ignored it all at once, shopkeepers took a break, and infrequent joggers ran out of breath. Host to a dozen antique statues, a thousand pigeons, fifteen swans, and, lastly, the park's warden.

Held in the hands of the Lombard-Chatons family for three generations, the current warden of Monceau was a seven feet tall, broad-shouldered man named Patrice. A good-looking young guy with a quick mind and a sharp eye, he was charming to a fault. Keeping a peaceful reign over the ancestral kingdom, the warden played his unofficial role as Paris' listener. People flocked to Patrice for issues far beyond the concerns of the park, horticultural advice, or neighborly quarrels. He was known to always be open for a chat and his unabashedly honest opinion.

As it goes, people liked to speculate about Patrice's calm

demeanor. One could only assume that it unsettled them to have someone so settled in the middle of their hectic lives. He had to be hiding something. There were stories about him running a secret cult or being a voodoo master - a reference to his Haitian heritage. Julie paid close attention to these stories and had tried to find any proof by observing the warden. While she liked the idea of these stories to be true and all of his strength and charm being confined by the same exploitations as the rest of the world, she never found them to be more than pure speculation. The only thing odd about Patrice was his shameless kindness. Julie knew it was, too, his energy that she felt inside Monceau.

Patrice was an enthusiastic and ruthlessly fair observer of every visitor in the park. Even when he seemed to be nodding along, lost in thought, he was aware of all ongoings. Indeed, Patrice seemed to have eyes on everything in Monceau at all times, able to pick up any abnormality through the thick chaos of school children and suited flaneurs. Julie knew the moment she spied him through the black bars of the outer fence that Maman and she were not going to sneak by unnoticed. They had just walked through the gate of the park.

Maman noticed Patrice as well and gave a stronger tuck to the bag containing Julie. She greeted the warden, who was standing with his back and looking occupied. Patrice replied with an absent "*Bonjour*," followed by an immediate and strong "One moment, madame!"

Maman stopped and caught her breath.

"Yes?" she said, quietly.

"What's all the hurry for, madame? Are you late for something?"

Maman probably hoped that he wasn't talking to her but turned around slowly to see Patrice's famous smile gleaming back at them.

"Ah … no … you see …" Maman hesitated. "Never too old for a quick stroll."

"Are you … is that a cat in your bag, madame?" Patrice asked. He was pointing at Julie's head.

"Oh, it's Julie … I mean … it's my … she asked me to take her …"

"Madame, are you aware that all pets need to be on a leash in Monceau?" Patrice threw a thumb over his shoulder to a sign hanging by the stone building of the entrance. "There are other animals in this park that might be in danger from your cat or might even put it in danger!"

"Yes, of course, Patrice! You know … I won't even let her out of my arms!"

"Won't let her out of your arms? Then why did you bring her?" Patrice had a chuckle in his voice.

Maman was quiet for a second. She looked down at Julie for help, but Julie looked at the warden. The park wasn't too crowded and their interaction attracted only a few curious glances. Patrice took a step toward them, wearing an amused expression, knowing that the situation was under his control. Julie thought it wisest to stay motionless.

"Madame, I would kindly ask you to leave the park if you don't have a leash for your cat. It's for her own safety." Patrice gestured toward the gate again. Just as he did, he looked to the side and froze, his face softened and the corners of his mouth loosened to a faint smile. His glance stayed fixated at the entrance.

"There you are!" a voice shouted from afar.

Maman jolted as Julie wrestled her arm to see who it was, even though she knew already. A tattooed brunette in a dark blue summer dress was skipping at them through the gate. She passed the rotunda and had swiftly joined the trio in the park. It was Anya.

Julie let out a jubilant cry when she saw her sister. It startled Maman. She tried to muffle Julie, but Patrice had already turned around looking bewildered from hearing another voice. Maman rubbed her throat demonstratively. Patrice stared at her under a raised eyebrow but quickly returned his gaze to Anya, who was twirling her dress, herself looking for where the source of the cry. Patrice seemed to be more captivated by the twirling than anything else. It was as if he recognized Anya.

"Bonjour, mademoiselle. Are you with madame?" he asked her.

Anya smiled at his address but kept scanning around. She looked at Julie, whom Maman kept half-hidden in the bag under her right arm.

"Bonjour, Patrice. Yes, this is my mother," she replied almost robotically, without breaking eye contact with Julie.

"Ah! Great! Well, then maybe you can help me explain why we can't have her cat in the park without a leash."

"What? Who puts cats on a leash?" Anya broke her eye contact with the cat, turned to Patrice, and lodged her hands on her hips.

"Mademoiselle, it's a rule of the park," explained Patrice. "I am not asking anyone to do it by force. It's for their own safety. We had a dog here yesterday—"

"You think of animals as some sort of slaves to us?" Anya interrupted him.

Patrice paused and took a deep breath before he continued.

"No, mademoiselle, this has nothing to do with what I think—"

"Aren't you a man of nature?"

"I am…" Patrice wore a nervous smile.

"Aren't you supposed to protect the animals and plants from us humans? These poor little creatures running all over your park and here you are, forbidding a little kitty to roam. We should be the ones on leashes for what we have done to this earth. Always shaping the environment around us. Is that what you want? Do you just want to create a perfect little universe for all humans?"

Patrice took another deep breath.

"Are you about done? I am the warden of this park." He spoke softly. "You are right - I am a man of nature. That is why I sometimes have to adhere to rules that are older and wiser than me."

"I think no one could be wiser than those of us who live now," Anya said.

Julie observed the exchange appear out of thin air, as so often with Anya. Maman stayed quiet too.

Patrice smiled and quickly lightened his expression again. Julie saw his concern morph into admiration of the young girl in front of him. Anyone else might have been put off by Anya's overt exclamation, but he took it with ease. That's when Julie remembered that Anya had mentioned crossing paths with Patrice recently. Julie tried to piece together the details of that story. It happened just after she had come back from visiting Ben in Amsterdam. Anya asked her to meet at *Café Brest* after work under the excuse that things with Victor hadn't worked out. There was more. Anya said that she wasn't feeling very well and was having something of a panic attack. Worse than usual. Julie knew that her sister needed to share, unlike herself, who would have done better being enclosed in a room for half a decade. It wasn't the first time Anya told her about an episode and Julie had always been impressed by her ability to voice them to her. She made it look so easy to put her thoughts into words and her words into action. Julie was able to piece the story back together: Anya told her that she ran into Monceau the night before they met at *Café Brest*. The voices wouldn't stop scraping against the splicing wheel of her mind. Those were Anya's words. She looked for any distraction, but none of her roommates were home, and so she walked out of the house. By the time she got to the park, she saw that Patrice had already begun to close it, but ran inside anyway. She took a sharp turn at the entrance and hid behind a big oak tree that reached over into the garden of the Catholic school. There she sat on the side of the stem facing the fence and kept talking to herself. It was something she often did. Anya told Julie that she didn't know how long she spent behind that tree or how it had suddenly become dark. There were noises in between her silent suffering, crunching sounds of footsteps stepping onto mulch, and a wind that sounded like a calm human voice. It took her a long time to get up, and when she did, she turned to a completely silent, dark-gold park. She walked back toward the same gate she entered through and was surprised to find one of the little doors unlocked. Anya walked through it and had almost turned the corner before she saw the gate being locked again by a tall shadow. She swore to Julie that it had been Patrice. Julie remembered Anya's tone of affection when she spoke his name.

Indeed, Patrice and Anya seemed to share more than met the eye in their standoff in Monceau. The short silence between them wasn't heavy and was soon completely broken by a smile from Patrice and then from Anya. Patrice took half a step aside and seemed to have started working on something in his head, moving his eyes from side-to-side, and then finally turning back to the group. He snapped back looking directly at Anya.

"All right," he said, scanning the two women and the cat in front of him. "Very well. Come on. Follow me."

Patrice took the first step to a brisk walk across the park's meadow behind him. Within a few steps, he was already halfway across the grass, stopped, and looked back. None of the ladies had moved. Maman was still clenching Julie and Anya didn't even have the time to take her arms off her hips.

"Come along. Don't be shy. You won't get a special invite," Patrice yelled from a distance. Some of the nearby parkgoers twisted their necks in passing.

Maman took the first step to follow, surprising both Julie and Anya.

"Maman, what are you doing?" Anya glared her down.

"It's all right, Anya. Let's do as Patrice says."

"Maman! What are you doing?" Anya repeated.

"Come on, Anya. Julie won't get off my back about this park."

"Julie? What?" Anya raised her eyebrows. "Where is she?"

Maman squinted her eyes and shook her head. "Ah … nothing. I mean … she'll be here." She opened her eyes again and pulled Anya to join her brisk walk.

"I thought we were going to meet her here," Anya mumbled as they moved closer to Patrice. "If he kills us, it's on you."

"Oh, stop it right now!" Maman spoke through her teeth.

"So, are you going to tell us where you're taking us, monsieur?" inquired Anya as they caught up with Patrice.

"Follow me. Right over here." Patrice waved a flat hand in front of them and pointed to the far end of the park, toward the eastern gate. Julie couldn't see where he was pointing to behind the broad green leaves of a maple tree in their way. The group made their way straight across the meadow until it was clear that they were heading for the old stone tower hidden in the corner of the park. Julie didn't remember it even being functional or open to the public.

The hexagonal tower by the eastern entrance looked like the little brother of the main tower by the northern gate. It was shorter, standing about twenty feet tall but much less visible, or in use. Ivy had overgrown its foundation and climbed over the bottom ten feet of its walls, masking most of the stone-framed windows. Only the bleached brown roof tiles were still showing clearly through the moss. There was a small fence encircling the ground where the grass and bushes had been unkept. Everything indicated to visitors that the tower was to be left alone. Indeed, it appeared almost like a natural object, blending in with the flora around it.

Julie felt an immediate urge to jump out into the tower's wild garden and explore. Her mother held on tight, sensing Julie's urge. Julie resorted to a meow. She turned her head around to see what Anya was doing. Her sister was shooting her estranged glances walking in the back of the group. Julie noticed that her dress fit her beautifully and she seemed to have gotten a new haircut. Her straight black hair now fell just past her jawline, a few inches shorter than the last time Julie saw her.

The trio was led through a creaking side gate, and Patrice walked up to the door of the tower. He reached into his pocket and took out a keychain containing no less than twenty keys, fondling the clinkers for a while, finding what looked like the oldest key in the bond, and inserting it into the old lock. The apparatus made a few loud clicks as Patrice turned the key. He turned his head to make sure no one was watching them. When the door finally unlocked, he was uncharacteristically careful to open the solid wood door.

"Let me go in first. Wait right here," he said and disappeared inside.

"He's preparing the chains and knives," Anya said.

"Oh, stop it! I know you're just as curious," Maman said.

Indeed, it was Julie that was exploding with curiosity. The urge to explore the garden had been multiplied exponentially with the opening of the rustic door. She heard Patrice's steps coming back down. He waved them in. Julie almost leapt out of Maman's lap in excitement. It forced Maman to take the first step, again.

"Calm now, for goodness' sake," she whispered to Julie.

As they stepped into the tower, a smell of old pots and wilting flowers surrounded them. It was dark, but Patrice must had opened a window upstairs as a glimmer of light came down from the top of the winding staircase. Patrice asked them to follow him up the stony steps. It was only then that Julie noticed something small and peeping in Patrice's arms. She wasn't sure if she saw right until the light coming from upstairs illuminated his torso.

"What are you holding, Patrice? Is that a ..." Anya said.

"Shhh ... please be quiet. Look!" said Patrice, pushing

the door to the first floor of the tower.

The group walked through the door and froze by the entrance.

The half-lit floor in front of them was crawling with cats left to right. All around the room, a myriad of miniature tigers was lying, sitting, or tumbling around, meeting the sound of the opening door with a few lazy meows. As soon as Patrice stepped in, a couple of cats walked up to him by curling their tails around his shins. Julie could count at least a dozen cats and a handful of kittens spotting the stone flooring of the tower, mostly lying on the comfy-looking carpets, hay, or woven wood furniture. There might have been more hiding in the shadow, she was not sure. Aside from the duo that greeted the arrivers, their entrance was met with an overwhelming indifference. Only a few kept staring at the door, while the rest returned to their feline business. Patrice walked to a patch of hay to put down the kitten he was holding.

Julie could not hold it any longer and used a careless loosening of Maman's grip to jump out of the bag, declaring her escape with a loud meow. She was filled with immediate regret as the fervor succumbed to fear. Her jump attracted curious looks from all her new kindred. Julie jumped back and cowered behind Maman's polka-dotted boots, realizing that she had not thought this through. Her jump had been courageous but preemptive. Luckily, the other cats remained as they were, turning away after they saw her hide.

"Patrice, are you serious?" Anya asked, standing slack-jawed.

Julie was relieved to have her draw the attention.

"What was it you said about slaves again?" Patrice had

a stupid grin on his face. "I feel like they control me more than I do them." He added a hearty laugh and walked to the three small windows to open the heavy drapes on them. "I guess we all…get to make a decision…like that." He opened each drape in sequence with his phrasing. Dust flew through the sunbeams that illuminated the room. "We get to make a lot of choices. When it comes to a fork in the road, we make our decision based on the condition we're thrown into."

"So, twenty cats were thrown at you?" Anya asked. "Is that why you decided to bring us in here? What in the world is going on? I feel like I'm in a movie. Maman! Hold on, Maman?!"

Anya waved at Maman to stand back, as she headed toward the haystack full of kittens. Julie made a last-second jump behind her sister's leg the moment her mother started moving.

"What?" Maman stopped in the middle of the room and shrugged. She turned to Patrice. "Patrice, do you mind if I pet your cuties?"

"Not at all, be my guest. They don't get nearly as much attention as they deserve. It's just me and some friends that come up here."

Maman approached the litter, surrounded by four adult cats. Some scattered as she came close, while the others perked up their heads and ears to pay close attention to what she was going to do. As Maman kneeled down and started to pet one of the gray kittens, the others quickly congregated to the non-threatening lady. The normality with which Maman treated the entire situation reminded Julie of her reaction earlier today.

"They were not thrown at me," Patrice said, turning to Anya. "These cats are strays that walked into the park over the years. We made sure that they have a home during the colder months, and in return, they give me company. Sometimes, when I am a little bit fed up with the world out there, they help me. I come here and talk to them. They help me with my demons."

"You see," Patrice continued, "they used to control me, those demons. They had me on a leash, if you will! They were there with me when I woke up in the morning, when I walked through Paris, walked through my park, everywhere! They used to control everything I did. Until I made this tower my meditative refuge. I come here and talk to them, and the cats listen. You know, I thought they would help me get rid of them, but I have found another thing, entirely. Something the cats taught me: Demons don't go away, you just get used to them. They become a part of you."

"You brought us in here to show us your demons? And your cats?" Anya asked. Julie could hear lingering disbelief in her voice.

Patrice laughed. "You're funny! Come, let's sit over there. We can talk for a moment, if you don't mind."

He pointed Anya to the semi-lit corner by the door of the room, which had a small table with two wooden chairs by its side. Anya looked down at the still-cowering Julie and then back at Patrice.

"I am sure she'll feel right at home," Patrice said, nodding his chin at Julie.

Anya turned to him, smiled, nodded, and walked over to the small table. Julie was left exposed once more and had to refocus on the cats. She felt encouraged by their calm nature and her sister's move to come out of hiding. She walked slowly across the room toward her mother.

As Patrice and Anya took a seat by the window. Julie sat down next to Maman, looking up at her. The low light exaggerated her wrinkles and Julie noticed how old she had become. The golden dusk of the room made her look like an oil painting. The oil painting of an old wife who stayed at home waiting for her husband in the ages of war. A feeling of loneliness crept up in Julie. It surprised her, as she had assumed it to be exclusively human.

Maman was playing with the kittens who were climbing all over her dark wool sweater at this point. Julie observed them letting off tiny peeps and squeaks as Maman was letting them bite her and climb over her arms. Julie rubbed her head against her mother's leg and received a pat on the head as well, purring.

Meanwhile, Patrice and Anya had started talking audibly.

"…will you tell me what bothers you now?" Patrice asked. He sounded more serious than earlier. "Why do you argue with yourself at night?"

"I thought I was the only one there." Anya lowered her voice.

"Nothing that happens in Monceau goes unnoticed by me." Patrice chuckled, leaning back in his chair.

"Speaking of which, don't you have a park to take care of?" Anya asked, avoiding eye contact with him.

Patrice chuckled, putting one hand on the side of his ribcage.

Anya didn't say anything. Julie saw that her sister felt uncomfortable without dismissing the talk. She held her hands in her lap and let her short black hair fall over the front of her face. Julie recognized an Anya struggling to find comfort in a strange place, something she usually managed much better. She knew that Anya had already allowed Patrice to come much closer than even he knew.

"Why are you hiding your fight?" Patrice proceeded, leaning over the small wooden table between the pair. "Who are you fighting against?" He pointed to Anya's head.

Anya kept her head lowered, looking at her own hands and then out of the window to her right. Julie was observing them closely, waiting for Anya to answer Patrice's question. Maman had slowed her petting, remaining quiet.

"That's my problem, Patrice. It's not any one person or thing," Anya said, breaking her silence. "It's an abstraction. Or at least I think it is…"

"An abstraction? What do you mean?"

"At least one."

Patrice gave off a hearty laugh. "Well, go on. Which one of them? Are you afraid of dying? Did some fool break your heart?"

"None of that," Anya replied.

There was a short silence. The pair at the table both looked at Maman, who had made a noise by adjusting her position to crossing her legs. Two of the tower-dwelling kittens climbed onto her lap.

Patrice took a breath and was about to speak when Anya surprised him by starting first, continuing to look out the window.

"All I want is my defining moment." Anya turned to him, moving her hands in a quick motion, but kept her voice down. "My life is full of these tiny, unimportant challenges. I know that I can achieve something great if I was ever put to the test, but it feels like I'm being left out. It just…I feel that I am constantly preoccupied with the thought of being inadequate. At the same time, I can't be by myself. I know that I need to be, but I am scared to be. The moment I come close to feeling like I am getting there, I latch on to whatever is closest, no matter if it hurts me or not. Maybe I'm simply undeserving. At the same time I am afraid to be normal and not do anything about it. I want my moment, but I fear that I have no right to have it."

Maman sat up straight while the kittens continued nibbling at her sweater with enough noise to compete with the low volume at which Anya was talking. Julie turned around to see what was happening and had a sudden desire to join the kittens. She forced herself to behave and continue to listen to the conversation of the room.

"You want to be alone?" Patrice asked.

"It's more complicated, Patrice. I think I need space. Space to make my own mistakes. I want to trace the ice twice or three times without someone else counting. Maybe I need it to break. Maybe I want it to break. I want to know that I can save myself. Does that make any sense, Patrice?"

Patrice leaned back in his chair and nodded. It was like listening to a chess player explain her strategy.

"We live in a world of extroverts, Patrice. It isn't made for cat-lovers." Anya grinned. "We need to be alone, from time to time, but they keep pulling us back. That's when we become addicted to their love, unable to let go. When you tell them, they don't understand, looking at you like you're from a different planet."

"I'm trying to follow you here. Are you saying your demons are others?" Patrice chuckled.

"Oh, come on, Patrice…" Anya looked up at Patrice, scoffed, and followed it with a shrug. "Well, maybe a little."

"We are all looking for a little bit of meaning," Patrice said.

"Yes, I know," Anya shrugged once more, "but I just know that I am destined for something great. I want to know that I am worth something. Something more than a chat-up line."

"You remind me of Duncan," Patrice said.

Anya raised her head.

"A folk tale hero from my island." Patrice started, adjusting his chair and laying his elbows on the table. "We tell many stories told about him. Usually to children before bed."

"No one remembers his actual name, but we always called him Duncan." Patrice continued, noticing Anya's interest. "He lived in one of the chiefdoms on Martinique long before the Europeans came. Had a great life with a beautiful wife and children, everyone envied him, but he was restless since his youth. Once his eldest son grew up, he went to his chief and asked him to let him set sail to a distant island in search of a hidden treasure legend among marooned sailors. Granting his plea, the chief agreed, giving him a ship and a crew, but Duncan had to prepare to leave immediately. He did not consult his wife or family and made it the honor of his life to go on this journey. His wife wept for days watching his boat disappear on the horizon."

"It took him years of adventures at sea to understand that he actually missed his wife. There came a point that the thought of return was the only thing that kept him going. By the time he found the hidden treasure, he was totally consumed by regret and could not bear to lift even one golden coin. When he saw it before him, he felt nothing, except the missing warmth of his wife's touch. He understood that he had been a fool and left the treasure where he found it, turning his sails back home. Alas, when he did reach familiar shores, his biggest fear had come true. His wife was taken by another man, and Duncan was left with nothing of his quest and a lost wife."

Patrice's story filled the room of the tower. Even the cats had remained quiet as his voice bounced off of the old walls.

"You should not let yourself be swept away by a search for glory. Are you even sure if you are ready for it? You should let your instinct guide you. Your great battle will come, don't worry. You won't need to look for it," Patrice added.

"I suppose," Anya said, batting her eyelashes with a smile. "Thank you."

Some cats started to meow. It was the ring to the end of the exchange. Before long, there was a choir of meows echoing in the tower. Patrice stood up and walked over to one of the woven baskets by the door, pulling out a pack of dry food and pouring it into dozen bowls that lined the wall next to the little table. The noise of the food hitting the metal bowls set most of the room in motion. Almost all four-footed animals of the rooms congregated to the wall. Julie too felt hungry but was still too shy to join the other cats in this approach. She did hope that they would leave something for her to eat. Meanwhile, Patrice packed the food away and held still between the door and where

Anya was sitting, with his hands on his hips, overlooking the room. He turned back to Anya again, who was back to looking out of her little window.

"I am a slave to them as they are slaves to me. You are absolutely right." He laughed and then turned to Maman. "And now I do have to go back to the tending the park. You are welcome, enjoy the Lombard-Chatons quarters of Monceau until I have to close. I can't let you go out in the park, but can stay here until I close, if you want."

He put his hand on the door handle and was ready to leave but froze.

"One more thing, Anya." He turned back around. "We should ... well, I ... hmm. Never mind. I'll see you later."

He smiled shyly and opened the door.

"Wait, Patrice." Maman stood up. "I'll walk out with you for a second. Anya, wait here, I'll be right back."

Patrice gave Maman a silent nod and waved her to pass in front of him. He gave one last smile to Anya before stepping out and shutting the door to the room.

The moment the door closed behind Patrice, Julie turned to see what her sister was doing. Anya was peering out of the window and seemed to be in deep thought. Julie wanted to say something to her but felt a stronger curiosity toward something else. The cats recaptured her attention, and Julie knew that this was her moment to learn more about her new kin. After spending the entire day locked in her studio daydreaming about what her new existence was about, she couldn't have expected to find the answer in an abandoned tower in Monceau. Her excitement had been building up with every movement and noise she saw the cats make. Anya had to wait.

The evening light had dimmed the room into an orange twilight. The cats that had finished dinner returned to nestle in the last sunny spots on the other side of the room, atop, or around three wooden stools. The rest laid down in the hay next to Julie or on the patches of old carpets. None of them paid much attention to the nervous newcomer. There were many questions on Julie's mind, but she decided to remain cautious. She was worried about making a wrong move or to seem too strange, still. She waited for the last cat to move away from the bowls to walk over and see if there was anything left for her to eat. Following her nose, she found a few nibbles that had spilled over the edges, munching them up with as little noise as possible. As she finished, she looked for a better vantage point to observe the room, moving closer to Anya, facing the room from the direction of the window that let in the sunlight.

When she had first looked inside the tower's room, Julie was overwhelmed by the number of tails and ears around the room, melting into and over each other in the hexagon.

A panicked eye doesn't catch the details. Making sense of the room felt as if she was trying to recognize a crowd in a theater, at night, from behind.

It was during the conversation between Patrice and her sister that Julie had begun to notice some distinctions, first in size and then in color. Most of the cats were some variation of black, gray, or white. None ginger, like herself.

A black cat with one white paw sat on top of one of the stools by the wall. The way she lay on her side made her look regal, returning Julie's studying eye with a piercing stare. In contrast to the other two cats that lay on the other two stools, she was not relaxed. Something of an old neighborhood lady, overlooking her street, monitoring any incessant loitering. A gray cat that sat down where Maman had been playing with the kittens started tumbling around. He was whirling up the hay and animating the kittens, who looked nappy after their dinner. A teenage brother with a little too much energy. Half hidden in the shadow, a white cat sat on a piece of ripped carpet next to the door. The cat ogled Julie for a moment, then yawned and turned around to look to the black cat on the stool. An informer, possibly. Julie wondered if she had a name, if any of them had names.

"So, you're the cat that Maman brought along."

Anya's voice broke Julie's concentration. Julie jerked her head around in time to see her sister kneel down from her chair and reach out her hand to pet her.

"I didn't know Maman had a cat." Anya spoke calmly. "Such beautiful ginger fur you have. I wonder what your name is." She stopped her petting and smiled. "You know, I have a feeling I could guess it! With such a recognizable expression and scream and those eyes, I would say your name is … Julie?"

Julie looked up at Anya and rolled to her side. Anya had on a big smile, wiping her face from the dust in the room.

"Anya!" said Julie.

"Ha! It really *is* you!" Anya's eyes widened with excitement. She bent down to give Julie a kiss on the nose. "And you can speak? How is this possible?"

Julie purred from Anya's kiss. "Yes, I know … but how did you recognize me?"

"Julie …! Of course I recognized you," Anya replied. "I knew it the moment I saw you in Maman's bag. I thought I was hearing voices when I saw Maman was hiding you under her arm! She sounded so strange over the phone, asking to come meet her because of something that happened to you. I was so worried. I never would've guessed that you turned into a cat!"

"I was so happy to see you finally. You have no idea," Julie said, still purring from her sister's scratches. "You wouldn't believe how Maman reacted. She was ready to blame me for this."

"I believe it." Anya laughed.

She made it seem as if she had just found Julie in a game of hide-and-seek, not transformed into a different species. Her dark blue dress looked black in the dimming light of the room. She sat with both her legs bent to one side, slouching a bit, and the air feeling heavy around her. Julie could sense that something wasn't right. Just then, Julie noticed that it wasn't dust that Anya had wiped away from her face. A bit of mascara was left smudged around her sister's eyes. Anya had been crying. Julie walked onto Anya's lap and put her head against her sister's chest. It was the closest she could do to giving her a hug.

"Why didn't Maman say anything on the phone. I would have come quicker!" Anya returned the hug by nudging her face against Julie's. "You're so fuzzy and cute! How did this happen? You have to explain everything to me! Start from the beginning!"

"I don't know what to tell you, Anya," Julie said, looking up at her sister. "I woke up without a bother on my mind, I look in the mirror, and see that I'm a cat. It was as much a surprise to me then as it is to you now. I am afraid I don't know any more myself." She licked her paw.

"Stop that! You're too cute!" exclaimed Anya. "Do you think you can teach me? Maybe I could become a cat, too! We could become the traveling cat sisters of France!"

"I don't know anyone besides you who would volunteer to be turned into a cat," Julie said.

"Oh, shush," Anya responded, petting Julie in her lap. "Who wouldn't love that? It sounds like a fairytale." Anya made big eyes at her sister, then adding "Tell me what it's like! How does it feel?"

"Not any different, to be honest," Julie replied and felt a twist in her stomach as she said it. Her sister had been the first person to ask her how she felt that day. Julie scanned her sister's face once more and saw her bright smile that reminding her of their father's. "Well, maybe a little different," Julie admitted.

"It has to be different than being a person!" Anya laughed.

"The fur takes a while to get used to," Julie replied. "It's quite itchy. Oh, and I'm hungry all the time! I feel famished again already! That is really all I can think of…Anya?

What are you thinking about?"

Anya kept petting Julie's head but had tilted her head to the side while Julie was talking. She stayed quiet for a bit, looking back at Julie and inspecting her. "Why a cat?" she asked. "I'm just wondering. Why did you turn into a cat, specifically?"

"I don't know, Anya."

"If you ask me, I think it fits you." Anya leaned back and looked Julie up and down.

"How so?" Julie was surprised.

"I mean, in many ways, you were very much like a cat already. You're shy. You like being in your control, and prefer to be left alone. It makes sense. You're basically the same as before. Just smaller, furrier, on four legs, and with a tail."

"You thought I was like a cat before? You never told me that," Julie said.

"I never thought about it before, but now that I see it, I can't say I'm fully surprised. You were always the more calculated and mysterious one – those are cat qualities. I mean, you seem very comfortable in your new skin, already. I'm not sure I would have been. I'm too loud and clumsy for a cat. A small dog with a Napoleonic complex, maybe. Like Arnold."

Julie meowed at the thought of the dog.

"Wow, you can even do that! Well, of course! It's just too adorable!" Anya hopped in her seated position. "What are you going to do now? I mean, do you have a plan on what's next?"

"I barely had time to think about it, Anya. Ever since I woke up, it's been busier than my normal life."

"I can help! Let's try to work it out together. I mean, it

seems like a marvelous opportunity, seeing the world from a completely new perspective," Anya said.

Julie was ecstatic to hear that someone else saw her transformation that way, too.

"Alright. This is how I see your situation," Anya continued, shaping a rectangle with her fingers and squinting. "You are a cat. Do you want to stay a cat, and if yes, why? What could be your purpose as a cat? Maybe this is some divine intervention that is challenging you to go on some great epic fight. Like what we just talked about with Patrice." She pointed to the table.

"I don't know, Anya. To be honest, I don't think I had much of a purpose as a person. Why would I have one as a cat?"

"Maybe it's because you needed to find purpose, and since you couldn't as a human, you became a cat," Anya said.

"In that case my purpose has something to do with food," Julie replied. "You don't happen to have anything with you, do you? I would kill for some meat."

"I might be able to help." An unexpected voice spoke from the other side of the tower room.

Both sisters turned around. Julie jumped behind Anya. The voice had cut through their conversation and ended it abruptly. It was definitely someone human, but no one had entered the tower room.

"What was that?" Anya yelled to the other side. "Who is there?"

Julie stared at the wall that was lined by the three wooden stools. It had gotten much darker, but she could still see the black cat with the white paw unchanged on the top of the middle stool. Her yellow irises shone like light beams through the dusky room. Julie was captivated by her glance and at once afraid of it. She didn't want to believe that this menacing creature had just spoken. But then she did, again.

"No need to yell. I said I might be able to help you." The voice sounded female, but it was clearly coming from the black cat.

Julie hissed. Anya pulled back, and the sisters watched the black cat jump down from the stool, without breaking eye contact and walk straight toward them.

All the hairs on Julie's back stood up. As the yellow-eyed cat inched closer, Julie felt electric shocks bolting in her sides. She felt flashbacks of her days on the playground and let out a few more desperate hisses. The entire room tensed up with her, as the eyes of all the felines focused on the black cat with her. In a panic, she pressed herself against her sister as tightly as she could. Her back curled more with every step she saw the cat make.

Just as the cat was less than two feet away, the door to the room suddenly swung open. Maman stepped in, unable to keep the heavy wood from hitting back on the wall. The bang from the hit was so loud and unexpected that it set off a whirlwind in the tower.

All the cats jumped up from the scare. Julie jumped on her sister's back as Anya yelled in surprise. The black cat jumped as well, doubly scaring the cats that were lying in the hay. The kittens all twitched to a symphony of squeaks. For that moment, the room was cat pandemonium. All non-human life sought out the darkest spots of the tower, scattering all around the hexagon. Distressing meows were heard from every corner.

"Sorry, sorry, sorry...!" Maman's words faded in the agitation. Her attempts to soothe the chaos were overheard.

Julie's heart beat at an alarming rate. Everything had happened so quickly that she didn't realize how she had ended up on her sister's shoulder.

"What the hell, Maman?" Anya implored. She was struggling with holding Julie on her shoulder as she stood up. "Let me light up the candles. I can't see anything. Ow! Careful, Julie. That hurts!" Anya screamed as Julie clawed into her shoulder, trying not to fall off.

"Let me put you down. I can't even see where I'm stepping," Anya said, grabbing Julie and putting her down next to her. Julie wanted to protest the handling but was too petrified to resist. She was still scanning the room, looking for the presence or even outlines of the black cat with the yellow eyes.

Anya moved toward the table and fondled with her matches, lighting the two wax candles on top of it. She left one on the table and moved the other one down to the floor next to Julie. The flickering light changed the energy of the room. Everything reverted to a serene setting by the sways of the little flame. The bang of the door and the subsequent pandemonium moved into the memory of a past scene of this tower, no longer relevant. Maman walked over to her daughters and sat down next to them as if nothing happened. Before she could say anything, however, Julie saw a movement out of the shadows of the hexagon. The black cat was the first to step out of the dark, walking up to the group, taking a seat on the other side of the candle, and turning to Maman with a steely voice.

"You enjoy scaring everyone, do you?" she said.

Maman, who had been carrying a face of utmost guilt, peeled her eyes and looked dumbstruck. It remained on her for a second and then slowly began to change to a face of confusion. Finally, she looked embarrassed. Considering the lightness with which she had taken Julie's transformation, Maman's face was remarkably expressive.

The cat's glance panned away from Maman, over Anya, and landed on Julie. "You must be very new to this. I can tell. I remember those days … and my first food cravings."

Julie tried to keep herself together, but all she managed to let out was a soft "what?"

The black cat had a satisfied smirk on her face and her eyes twinkled. She was sitting in front of them, her tail wrapped around her side and dropping at the front, with the light of the candle flickering off of her black fur. Julie did know whether to trust her or to attack her.

"Not to worry. It gets easier with time," the black cat continued.

"How can you tell?" Julie asked, pulling herself together. "How can you tell I am new ... to this?"

"How long has it been for you since you turned into a cat?" the black cat asked. "A month, maybe two?"

"Today."

"Today?! Well, in that case, you are doing very well! I barely made it out of bed on my first day!" She raised her nose at Maman. "I am guessing this is your family?"

"Yes ... yes, they are. My sister, Anya, and my mother," Julie replied.

"What is your name?" the cat asked.

"Julie."

The cat paused, inspecting the group in front of her. Anya had put her arm around Julie, while Maman was sitting on her knees behind them. The family must have portrayed an interesting sight for the cat, Julie thought. She felt Anya's restraint tighten.

"Excuse me," Anya said, clearing her throat. "*Who* are *you?*"

"My name is Appoline," the cat replied, without hesitation. "I am sure you have as many questions for me as I have for you. For my part, firstly, I have to admit that after all these years, I never thought I would meet another one like me."

"Another one?" Anya interjected. Her voice sounded protective, and her grasp tightened even more.

"A new-cat, transformed, a human stray," the cat replied briskly. "It seems that your sister and I were met with the same fate. Just like her, I was once human, until one day I - *abracadabra* - I was a cat. That was about five winters ago. Ever since then, this is me." Appoline licked one of her paws without breaking eye contact with Anya.

"Oh my..." Maman gasped in the background.

Anya looked at Julie, raising her eyebrows. Julie wasn't sure what to say or feel at this point. She was still deciding what to make of Appoline after hearing her speak. At close range and in the candlelight, her eyes became less menacing, and her initially smug look gave way to a sort of candor. She was moving her tail slowly left to right in front of her paws, just like Julie had learned to do in the mirror in the morning. Her voice sounded hoarse, and Julie guessed that she was likely the same age as her mother in human terms.

"You have been a cat for five years?" Julie asked, leaning forward to get out of Anya's arms.

"Six this November! And those are human years..." Appoline answered. She made a pause before continuing. "I don't mean to be the bearer of bad news, but I suppose you'll find out sooner or later: You are now in a cat's body, you'll age like a cat. But don't worry! There are a lot of upsides to it. I mean, I should be sixty-five by now, but I can still climb a tree or sprint across a park! I'm not sure about the nine lives, I have to tell you. But I am starting to believe it."

126

"Sixty-five…?" Julie muttered to herself. "Grow old…"

"It's not bad," continued Appoline. "You sort of forget it after a while. At least you're rid of all those worries that matter to people. You know, running after life, stuck on a hamster wheel. Always on the search for something in pointless pursuits. No, it's almost liberating." She shook her head. "My few years as a cat have been long enough to fill a person's life or two."

"But what have you been doing all this time?" Anya asked. "Didn't you want to find out how this happened to you?"

"Of course!" Appoline replied. She took one step closer to them. "It was the first thing I tried to find out once I understood that I wasn't dreaming. I was furious. I wanted to get back into my old self. In fact, I spent an entire year trying to find a way to get back. I tried everything. I asked my family, friends, doctors, and vets, but none could help me. After months of trying, I even started looking for un-conventional solutions."

Appoline had gotten up and started pacing in front of the candle while telling her story. At one point, she held still and glanced around to look at the other cats. Julie saw that they were barely paying attention, except for the white informer cat that was staring back at them emptily. "Don't worry. She might understand, but she was never human," said Appoline when she noticed Julie's questioning look.

"She understands?" Julie asked, feeling a lump building in the back of her throat.

"Of course. What did you think?" Appoline laughed. "All cats understand humans."

"I knew it!" Maman breathed into the conversation.

"Wait, hold on." Anya refocused. "What do you mean by unconventional solutions?"

"That's when I became desperate!" Appoline continued. "I panicked, and I didn't want to accept what had happened to me. I was obsessed with finding a way back. Everyone who I consulted was either too scared or incapable to help me. I became a nuisance for my family and friends, a shame to be around. They preferred to forget that I ever existed. After a while, I hate to admit it, but I started to believe it. I believed that I might not be real." Appoline's black fur stood up on her back, and her voice became rougher. "People thought I was the devil herself" Appoline sat down and sank her head.

Julie turned her head from a sound coming from behind her. She saw Maman running her fingers through her hair and looking at the door. Julie had only moments to wonder what her fidgety before Appoline proceeded.

"I saw voodoo doctors and wizards and fortune tellers, astrologists, and wiccans. I was never a believer in their powers, but it's funny how the absurd becomes reasonable within the absurd. As if our world didn't have enough crazy people … At least they tried to help! I received every counter-incantation and magical potion I could get my paws on. All failed, as you see in the proof in front of you. The last one, a German druid, almost poisoned me to death. That was when I decided to give up on trying to turn back."

Appoline took a deep breath and turned to Julie. "I think that deep down, I knew that nothing would work from the very first day. The same feeling you are having now, Julie. The feeling that there is nothing to be done. I just did not know how to accept it. I kept fighting for longer than I should have."

The black cat sat back down, her back fur flattened, and her voice soothed. The discomfort her own story had brought on her subsided and her serene elegance took its place again.

"So, you gave up?" Anya asked.

"In the end, I wouldn't say that I gave up. I just accepted this new life and stopped questioning it. I stopped feeling sorry for myself. You know, it's actually not bad to be a cat in Paris. I get my food from Patrice and get to stroll through the city by night. Montmartre just around the corner. Hard to complain … apart from the occasional hairball."

Julie walked past Anya's legs and took a seat in front of her knees, face to face with Appoline.

"I keep to myself and decide when to be seen and when not to be seen," Appoline continued. "I don't have any social responsibilities. I don't need to care for others and don't have to depend on them in return."

A light breeze crossed the room and froze the conversation. Julie took a deep breath in the brief stillness. She had dissected every word Appoline had said until now.

"That's it?" Julie broke her silence, looking at the ground in front of Appoline. "Now, you're just happy and alone?"

"Yes," she replied, adding, "I have this tower and an entire city beyond. I live without obsession or status. What do you think? Not bad, right?"

Julie looked to the ground, feeling her sister's eyes on the back of her furry head.

"But I was never unhappy with people," Julie said.

"You were not?" Appoline asked, sounding surprised.

"I just wanted to leave Paris for a day. That's all I wanted.

To be left alone for a little while but not forever. I don't want to lose every last bit of humanity. I was happy...," Julie replied.

"If you were happy, then why did you turn into a cat?" Appoline asked.

Julie did not have an answer.

"You wanted to leave Paris?" Anya asked. Julie looked up at her sister. "You never told me."

"It was something that came to mind today," Julie replied, wanting to move on from the conversation. She looked back at the yellow eyes, still beaming at her across the candlelight. It was as if the room around them had emptied, four lonesome pairs of eyes around the burning wax. The other cats had disappeared and with them the room. Gone was the old warden tower, its walls and Monceau and Paris. Julie saw herself from the outside, just like she did when she was a child, in the middle of this tiny world.

"I am fine with what I have ... or had." Julie spoke through her teeth, directing it at anyone who listened, feeling increasingly frustrated. "Why does everything always have to have meaning? Why does everyone worry so much about what I do? I live a mediocre life and don't complain. Up until this morning, I didn't think I could care any less about all of this, but here we are!"

Another, stronger breeze came through the window and almost extinguished the fire.

"I think you are confused," Appoline said, flashing her yellow irises at Julie once more. "I was too in the beginning. You're just too scared to grasp it now, but you'll get there."

Julie turned to her mother by instinct, who had stayed

uncharacteristically quiet. Her face was even more tired than it was before. There was an emptiness in her that made her look peaceful as if her mind had been erased. A new painting.

"It's Papa, isn't it?" Anya interrupted the silence.

"What?" Julie jumped away from her sister.

"Oh no, Anya." Maman spoke up. Her voice was soft.

"I know how close you two were," Anya added.

"No! It has nothing to do with him," Julie said.

"Are you sure?" Anya asked again.

"Yes!" Julie turned to Appoline. "And I'm not confused. I am certain that I don't want to disappear completely." She felt an urge to jump out of the nearest window.

"Then maybe you are still more human than cat." Appoline didn't even blink at the change of tone in everyone's voice.

"Maman, can we go? Please?" Julie walked up to her mother.

Maman sprang to her feet as if she had been waiting for the request. She had discomfort written all over her face and walked straight for the door.

"Yes, let's leave!" she said.

Anya didn't say anything but also hastened to her feet. Appoline moved nothing but her ears.

Julie sprinted to the door and ran out through the crack as soon as Maman opened it. She slid downstairs to find the tower door shut.

"Please open the door," Julie yelled up the staircase.

"Are you going to run away?" asked Mama, approaching.

"Not if you don't open the door."

"Good luck, Julie. I hope we'll meet again." Julie heard

Appoline's voice from a distance, unsure whether she actually heard it or if she was imagining it.

Her thoughts raced ahead of her. Julie couldn't control a feeling of incredible loneliness strangling her. Whether it was by Anya's words or intuition, she wished for her father to be there and take her away, to end this day.

Before Maman opened the door, she tried to grab Julie to put her back in the bag, but Julie wouldn't go. Julie clawed, bit, wheezed, and hissed, but Maman held against it. She took her daughter in a strong grip around the sides and lifted her under her arm.

"Please, Julie, no, no, no!" Maman implored, struggling to calm her. "Don't do this…! Let's just get out of the park together."

Julie heard the pleading tone in her voice. She wanted to listen but couldn't see beyond the two hollow yellow circles piercing at her. As soon as Maman opened the door, she leapt out of Maman's arms and landed in the grass lawn in front of the tower. She made for cover as fast as she could and didn't turn around, aiming to get as far as possible without being seen. Dodging the branches and scattered rubbish, Julie didn't realize how fast she reached the eastern gate. She ran through it, onto the street and dodged under a parked car, crawling behind one of the front wheels, feeling her heart pounding through her chest. Screams of "Julie!" sounded from the park, each scream like fork against the porcelain. Julie could only see shades, nothing was in focus. Her vision pulsated.

J ulie waited for what felt like hours. She didn't pay attention to the footsteps around the car or the opening and closing of doors on the street. She didn't hear any more voices calling her name or anyone at all. Even Appoline's yellow eyes had fled her memory. Julie's mind had become blank in anger and fear. She felt broken. One part of her wanted to scream, and the other wanted to suffocate. She had been riding the train for so long, she had forgotten this stop had to be coming. She stared at the curb of the pavement in front of her and felt its smooth edge. The gray surface of the stone peaked back at her in kind, resolute and comforting. Julie felt the end of her streak. She was ready to cry. Her face contracted and her eyes closed, but nothing came out. She thought of Anya's smudged mascara and felt all emotion make way for sadness but couldn't drown it. Not even a drop on her furry cheeks. She couldn't. Now that she wanted to, it was too late; cats couldn't cry.

Julie's mind emptied by the time she crawled out of the car. She had no place to be or direction in mind but felt the need to move, so she started by crawling from underneath one parked car to the next. Allowing her new instincts to take control, she was letting her body be guided onward. They took her further out of the side road, across the *Boulevard Malesherbes* and toward the florist on the corner of *Boulevard de Courcelles*. The owner of the store was moving his merchandise back inside for the night while his wooden patio reflected the reddish evening sky from the dripping flowerpots hanging over its veranda. Julie approached the front. The regular drips distracted her into a meditative state, she even allowed a few drops to fall on her head. The water tasted flowery and reminded her of her grandmother's garden in Normandy. Julie shook her head.

The sidewalk was scarcely populated for the time of day. Of the few pedestrians, some bent down to try to pet Julie; others did not notice her until it was too late and had to turn their necks. Julie stayed close to the walls of the tall buildings, turning corners on each of the entrances to avoid being seen.

Atop the railway bridge of *Métro Rome*, a young family caught Julie's eye. A young boy dashed around his parents, holding a galette in his right hand and flinging it around carelessly. At the stoplight, an unexpected stop by the father made the snack fly out of his hand and land in the bushes by the street. The boy cried for his tainted food, but the father grabbed him to cross the street. Julie's dinner was served.

As Julie reached the bustling crossroad of *Place de Clichy*, she continued to follow her gut up the boulevard, entering the alley next to *The Harp*, facing the Montmartre cemetery. Julie squeezed between the black bars of the entrance gate and trotted up the paths to the old graveyard. The stacked mausoleums looked homely. Curiosity overcame her, not unlike seeing her studio's furniture in the morning, and Julie felt a sense of hospitality in being among the deceased. She climbed around the weather-worn tombstones until she found the opened mausoleum of one Bertrand de Randonnée-Loin, which had noticed from down the path. She could not have known what Bertrand had done in his life to have deserved this structure, but neither would he have known for it to become a lost cat's shelter many years later. Seven columns surrounded an interior filled with three levels of shelves with names of other relatives of Bertrand's family. Julie jumped up and down the shelves and felt it right to tumble on the floor, which had the drawing of a religious figure she didn't recognize. Dust flew up from the ground, and for a split-second, Julie swore to see a shadow walk up to the entrance. She ran out of the mausoleum with her head down and jumped to the neighboring tombstone and the next, reaching the exit of the cemetery right in front of the *Hôtel Terrace*.

It was the height of the evening, and Montmartre's streets were crowded. Sidewalks were filled with risky romances seated by the tables too small for their personalities. Each table leaned a little further into the street as if to tempt fate with each inch of usable space. Julie tried to stay hidden as she squeezed between the chairs and legs but couldn't evade some joyous screams of "*Putain*! A cat! A ginger cat!".

Her instincts were leading her to the stairs of Montmartre. It surprised her not to have thought of it earlier. These endless stairs had always been loaded by sentiments of an escape, a route out of the smoggy spoon of the city. Julie reached the stairs at the top of *Rue des Trois Frères* and looked up. The cloudless sky had become dark purple as the streetlamps turned on to illuminate the facades of the slanted buildings. There was the smell of wine and food in the air and no one seemed to care about the stray anymore.

At the top of the stairs, at the café, *Chez Marie*, more couples lined the sidewalk in their tiny tables and chairs. The illuminated red and white café sign swung its open arms over the evening scene, and the lights inside splashed a golden color onto the cobbled street. As Julie approached diagonally, she smelled roasting fish and something else, a more familiar smell, one she didn't recognize at first but got an unexpected jolt from. It ran through her, not unlike the warning intuition she felt in the tower. She tried to ignore it but couldn't control her growing anxiety. It was when she was a few feet away from the café that she realized what it was, when it was already too late. The smell instantly connected with the voice and sight of someone whom Julie could not have expected. Sitting cross-legged and wearing a fitting casual suit of blue and gray was Ben. Her Ben. At one of the tables facing away from *Rue Gabrielle*. Sitting next to him, an attractive young woman giggled at something he said, holding a glass of white wine between two fingers and her palm. The woman didn't look unlike Anya and somehow distinctly Parisian, wearing a small black dress and only the hint of red lipstick. Ben and she were involved in a passionate display of affection, touching and leaning into each other like two tied dinghies bobbing against each other in the waves. Julie watched them interrupt their eye contact only to exchange whimsical smiles and then shyly glance away. Caught in a stupor, Julie held still by the curb where the two love birds did not seem to notice her.

"…it's delicious, isn't it?" Ben asked his company. "The weather couldn't be nicer either. We're lucky to get a table outside."

"Can I try some of yours?" the woman asked, taking a bite of the fish on Ben's plate.

"How do you like it?" he asked. His company nodded with a curious smile and giggled again.

Julie did not hear them say much more as Ben started to caress his partner's revealed shoulder and kiss it. He leaned back and met her eyes. They both held their heads back for a moment before the woman's body curved forward, closing her eyes and kissing him back on the lips.

A flash went through Julie and she saw Appoline's yellow irises again. They burnt through her and made her stomach turn to the thought of her naive stupidity. She could no longer look at the couple. A sharp noise sounded through the street, and Julie turned her head to see a group of four women coming out of a nearby bar. They approached the corner of *Chez Marie*, and Julie took their feet as cover to escape the night's theater of heart abuse. Following the group without thinking, she just wanted to keep moving again. At the top of *Rue Gabrielle*, she stopped and took one look back at the café. A jazz trumpet sounded from a distance and Julie gladly saw the couples outside morphed into an indistinguishable row of bodies. When Julie turned back around, the group of noisy women had disappeared as well, and she was left alone.

She could keep going, possibly forever, her mind was convinced, but her paws would not move anymore. Julie stood on the side of the street, watching the cobblestones reflect the moonlight. Night had fallen.

Julie was tired. She sat down by the footpath, hanging her head into her ginger coat, still in earshot of the café. Her first instinct was to go home, but when she tried to move, her legs faltered. She had to lie down. There were very few pedestrians in this part of Montmartre, and the light from the closest street lanterns did not reach her sorry figure. She was covered by the dark.

It seemed cruel to her that it all happened so quickly. Julie considered returning to the café to see if Ben was still there, maybe he was going to help her, or take care of her. But the image of him caressing his mistress, holding her hand, and kissing her neck revolted Julie. She remembered the last time they had met in Amsterdam and how she thought she had the upper hand, never allowing emotion to play a part in it, thinking it was all under her control.

It reminded her of another story from her father. About how Aphrodite had fallen in love with Ares, the god of war, even though she was meant to be with another. He told his daughters that in his life, he had never seen anyone be in love with the person they were meant for. There was no point in fighting the universe in matters as powerful as that. If such a cruel match is possible among the gods, then what are us mortals left with?

A sudden rush of energy went through Julie's body. At once, she jumped to her feet and started moving, running. She did not care where to as long as it was not after Ben, or anyone. She ran back down toward Pigalle. Her run was blind. She couldn't concentrate on the objects and people in front of her. Her heightened reflexes saving her from getting run over or kicked as she jumped over ledges and fences without stopping. Her eyes were open, but she couldn't see. Her mind raced through a hundred memories of her father in Normandy and running around in her grandmother's garden. She heard herself crying uncontrollably. Her whimpering meows flew off into the deaf alleys of Montmartre as she sprinted across its slanted streets.

She thought of her father's love and how he always understood her. She thought of Anya's relentless hope and how it made Maman jealous. Her family, a pillar of her existence, laid out in front of her like a dusty blueprint. Where had it been before?

Once the weight was taken by the tears, it became simple. It took a trivial series of processions to understand. There was no fanfare or grand battle like Anya wanted it. It wasn't a fight with a big adversary or teachings by a wise mentor as Julie had imagined it. It wasn't even her transformation into a cat. It was what she saw when the day came to an end.

Julie reached *Place Pigalle*, catching her breath under the seat of a bus stop. The Edith Piaf impersonator was still out singing in the middle of the square. Julie moved on without over-indulging in the powerful lines of "*non, je regrette rien.*" She dodged drunk tourists in their brightly colored shirts and was once again in front of *Folies Pigalle*, which she passed with Maman a few hours ago.

The exhaustion from her day pinnacled. Julie thought of Appoline and Patrice in his park. Maybe she should have stayed in the tower with her new kin. Maybe she would have overcome the initial scare. She passed the square at the top of *Rue des Martyrs*. The few who were still wandering the streets seemed to be returning home on full stomachs.

Among them, a family of four passed in front of Julie. In

the midst of her parents, a little girl was running toward the carousel in the middle of the square. Her red dress caught Julie's attention. It struck her as something out of place in the darkness of the evening. The dress gave the girl a pristine gleam around her as she was chasing her brother, screaming with joy and pinching her mother's dress as she ran around her. Everyone was caught up in her happiness as the father's chuckle echoed in the empty street.

Julie tried to remember the last time she had happily run toward something. It seemed as distant as any dream she would try to remember. The last song of the Edith Piaf impersonator came bellowing from a distance. It was "*Dans ma rue.*" Julie thought about the girl in the red dress one day understanding its lyrics. It would happen, one day, unexpectedly, and would seem like a most inescapable truth. She would wake up from a slumber and realize how its melody hid a cry waiting to be heard.

Julie slid down her nightly street. Getting close to her home, she spotted shadows filling the sidewalk in front of her building and slowed down her pace to see what was going on. She widened her eyes on the approach and recognized the two figures standing in front of number 54 immediately. Their difference in size and the proximity to each other made it comically obvious. The smaller one with short dark hair was moving around the sidewalk and extending her neck to look past the cars, while the much larger one leaned against the building with his hands in his pockets. They were Anya and Patrice.

Julie stepped away from the walls and into the light. Anya spied Julie, screamed, and ran toward her. Julie made no secret of being happy to see her sister either. She let off a few meows, jumped, and buried herself in Anya's arms as soon as she reached them. The last few tears that were lodged in her face wiped away against Anya's dress.

"Not a sight you see every day," Patrice said. He approached the hugging sisters.

Anya turned around with Julie in her arm. Her face shone in the night's light.

"Patrice, meet Julie. My sister," she said.

"Nice to be meet you, finally." Patrice chuckled. "I don't know why your mother didn't just introduce us in the park. Although, I guess I do."

He glanced at the sisters with a caring look and then made an affirmative nod. He walked over and gave Anya a kiss on the cheek.

"I leave you two, then," he said. "Call me tomorrow or if you need anything."

"Yes, thank you. I'll see you soon. Thank you for everything."

Patrice gave Julie a soft pet.

"Thank you," Julie said.

He gave them one more smile and nod before he turned on his heel and walked away. Julie watched her sister follow the man's departure and could see her missing him already, but then turning to her and giving her a nudge on the nose.

"Where were you?" she asked. Anya took Julie in one arm and reached into her pocket with the other. The smell of rain was in the air, and a few droplets started to speckle the street with darker shades. Anya took out Julie's set of apartment keys that Maman had taken earlier and opened the door.

"I had to go. I thought you'd understand," Julie replied.

"Yes. I really do. I just didn't expect it." Anya looked down at Julie before she walked upstairs. "Let's get inside, and I'll make us something to eat and drink. Patrice thought it would be a good idea to get some tuna for you in case you'd be back ..." She paused. "I am happy you came back."

Anya carried her sister up the six floors, and as soon as they entered the apartment, put her down on the bed. She walked into the kitchen to put on the kettle, opening the promised can, which filled the room with the smell of tasty fish. She put on a plate in front of Julie. The cat didn't hesitate, and Anya sat down next to her watching her eat.

"I was wondering..."

The kettle boiled, and Anya got up before finishing her sentence. Julie could smell the ginger lemon infusion mix with the smells of her studio. The rain had picked up and was now pattering against her old windows. Anya came back with the mug and shut the window in the bedroom

143

before sitting down on the bed herself, leaning against its backboard. She exhaled deeply.

"Did you really want to leave Paris?"

Julie lifted her head from the plate and looked at her sister.

"Yes, I did. I thought about it a lot," Julie said. Her phrase ended with a meow, which made Anya smile.

"OK, then. It's settled! We'll leave tomorrow!"

"What? Where?"

"I'm taking you out of Paris. We'll go to see Mami in Montebourg. She'll be happy!"

Julie looked in her sister's eyes. They were lit up with excitement and there was no space to convince her otherwise.

"Thank you, Anya," she replied.

Anya scooted down further on the bed and let her head fall on the pillow, rolling to her side. Julie could see that her sister's eyelids opened with a delay, as much as her own were starting to feel heavy. She walked across the bed and squeezed under her sister's elbow to cocoon her in a spot not far from where she had woken up in the morning. Anya continued to stroke her fur, and before she knew it, Julie had fallen into a deep sleep.

The following morning, on the 18th, Julie woke up by the sound of her alarm playing the morning radio. She had to stretch to reach the button for switching it off. Her movements felt strangely uncoordinated, nudging the gifted golden cat with her hand by accident. It waved its plastic arm with an absent smile. Julie looked at the time: it was 8 a.m.. Time to get ready for work.

I want to thank the many friends and family that have supported me and this work along the way. It is dedicated to you all and anyone else who finds it hard to fit in. I hope this book found you at the right time.

If you liked this novella, feel free to rate it on your preferred review website. It does a lot to support independent writers like myself.

To stay up to date on future projects or to send me a message, visit www.anatolischolz.com/contact.

Printed in Great Britain
by Amazon

43101142R00088